Mary Patricia King was born in Connemara.This is her first novel. She now lives in London England.

AISLING

by

Mary Patricia King

Grosvenor House
Publishing Limited

This book is published by
Grosvenor House Publishing Ltd
28-30 High Street, Guildford, Surrey, GU1 3EL.
www.grosvenorhousepublishing.co.uk

All characters in this publication are ficticious,except for the photographic images and any resemblance to real people, living or dead is purely coincidental.

A CIP record for this book
is available from the British Library

ISBN 978-1-908447-86-9

To my paternal grandmother Margaret McDonagh from whom I draw inspiration every day and

Éamonn
Noël
Seán
Rachel
David
Róisín

Maura McHugh was very tired now. She had walked at least one mile from her cousin's house where they talked about her going to America. There was another mile to walk to her home. It was the Summer of 1925 and so many people were leaving the country. She sat down on a rock at the foot of the Connemara Twelve Pins mountains, took off her sandals and rubbed her feet. She gazed across at the great stretches of heather and gorse and watched the setting sun as it threw up great splashes of colour – gold and pink, mingled with the blue of the sky.

As she bent over to rub her aching feet, her red-gold shoulder length hair gleamed in the setting sun and her blue eyes were wistful as she thought of going to America. "No more walking like this, when I get there" she thought, but Eóininń Bán might be along soon with his horse and cart. "What is this noise? Oh yes! It was Eóininń Bán's horse galloping along in full speed. Maura knew he would not stop now – he was going to the races. It was well known that when Eóininń Bán was going to the races there was a full moon. They passed where Maura was sitting. "Maura, I'm off to the races", he shouted and with that he was off down the road, standing in his cart, willing the horse along, with his red wool scarf and his fair hair flying, disappearing in a cloud of dust. Eóininń Bán had not changed much since their schooldays. He was always going somewhere in his imagination, Maura remembered as she watched him thunder past her.

Just as she got up to walk the rest of the journey home, she heard another sound _ not familiar this time. She looked back and saw a man driving a car at a very steady pace. The car stopped near where she was standing and a young man, with a shock of black wavy hair leaned forward towards her saying, “there’s a long road ahead, hop in”, Maura hesitated for a moment. “It’s a long road ahead alright” she agreed and “my feet are in a bad way”. The young man opened the car door and she slid in beside him. He started up the engine and soon they were cruising along amid the masses of fuchsia growing on both sides of the road. The young man looked quickly at Maura, “my name is John O’Dowd and I’m out here visiting my brother, who lives in Innisbeg, he’ll be picking me up in his boat from Stonebridge”. John was looking straight ahead and Maura looked at him shyly, taking note of his regular features and strong jaw line. She took a deep breath “we’re nearly there now _ my home is just around the next bend in the road”. Just then, Eóinin̍ Bán came tearing along the dusty road. John stopped the car.

“Who is that”? John asked as he turned and watched Eóinin̍ disappear into the distance.

‘Oh’ that’s Eóinin̍ Bán, he’s been to the races”, Maura responded calmly with a slight smile.

“What races?” John was looking perplexed.

“He goes to the races every time there’s a full moon.”

“Oh! I see! John relaxed and laughed out loud.

“Well, here we are, I can walk now – and thank you.”

John stopped the car, Maura got out and walked slowly towards the house – the little cottage where the smoke was curling up from the chimney. John called out "I don't know your name" 'Maura' she shouted back and waved goodbye.

John continued his journey towards Innisbeg. "Maura", he mused, with her red-gold hair and her soft voice and her frail little figure and her sore feet. "Poor Maura".

—∞—

It was twilight time when John arrived at Stonebridge. He parked the Ford Sedan and walked the short distance to the harbour where his brother, Páid, was waiting proudly in his boat - the Galway Hooker. Páid worked on his boat in all weathers, ferrying turf from the mainland to the various islands round about. "Great weather now "said Páid as John stepped on to the Hooker. Páid sailed the boat expertly towards Innisberg and his home. As they came near John could see the lights twinkling in the little houses on the island and smell the familiar smoke from the turf fires. John stepped ashore as Páid anchored the Hooker at the cove. They walked together the short distance to the cottage, John towering over his brother. "You'd like a mug of tea now after your journey," Páid was struggling with his words in the middle of a cough. John noticed that Páid had been coughing a lot during their short trip across the bay.

"How long have you had that cough? Ah! It's nothing Páid retorted, it's only a tickle in me throat."

He never liked to make a fuss. Once inside, Páid made two mugs of tea and handed one to John. They drank the tea in silence. John leaned over the left his empty mug on the table. He looked at Páid

"I'm thinking of going over to New York".

Yes, there's a lot of people going over there – they say it's a great place".

Páid got up and walked towards the bedroom next to the kitchen. He emerged after a few moments with the oil lamp. He turned up the wick, lit it and replaced the globe. He handed the lamp to John. "Here, take the lamp, your bed is ready in there" - nodding towards the bedroom without another word, he went into the other room behind the dresser.

John carried the oil lamp into the bedroom, its light casting eerie shadows on the whitewashed walls. He was tired. He had a long drive today. Soon he was drifting off to sleep – to dream – He was sitting with Maura in Eóinińn Bán's cart. The horse was galloping along throwing them together and all over the cart. As they journeyed through the rough terrain, which was typical of the Connemara roads, Eóinińn Bán was singing "we're all going to the races, to the races.....

Next morning was Sunday and John was awakened by the sun streaming through the small window which was without curtains, unlike when his mother lived there. In those days, the house was kept so beautifully – lace curtains always on the windows. Her husband, Colm O'Rourke spent his days with his companions in the currac, fishing and carrying turf from the mainland to the islands, until that fatal evening when the boat capsized in a raging storm. He and two of his companions were lost in that storm, although they had rowed across and were almost near the shore. None of the men could swim. In spite of all this Páid wanted to follow in his father's footsteps, and build a currac.

Three of his friends on the island helped and finally they built the boat. Kate, his mother, was distraught. Before she died she told them – "the sea has no mercy". After a few years of battling with strong winds and tides, rowing their currac with their cargo of turf, became such a struggle that they decided to invest in a hooker – the Galway or Connemara Hooker, as it is known, the name Hooker probably coming from the Dutch word HOEKER.

Besides, the local matchmaker had told them that a good reliable boat was needed to transport the batchelors from the main land to the islands in order to visit their brides-to-be. Men, mostly in middle age who decided that it was time now for them to settle down with a strong young woman from the islands. The matchmaker, carrying a bottle of Poitín, always accompanied the bachelors to meet their prospective brides and if their parents were willing and the dowry adequate the match was sealed with a glass or two of Poitín all round. There were times, however, when the young girl caught sight of her suitor, she declared that she was not interested and so, the suitor, matchmaker and crew returned to the boat and consoled each other with the Poitín, singing the joys of the single life, after all.

John and Páid ate a hearty breakfast and having cleared away the dishes they boarded the hooker and set sail towards the harbour, where they said their goodbyes. The brothers faced each other and shook hands. "I'm on my way to visit Martin and Honor in Cliften, John said as he stepped ashore. "Día leat"*{God be with you} Páid murmured and sailed away in the crisp morning air. John approached his parked car on the pier, started the engine and drove along the winding road to Cliften. He thought of Martin and Honor who were teachers now. They were married for just one year. They all had been friends for a long time – since their schooldays, in fact. John was the only son of John O'Dowd, the merchant who had become wealthy in the export business, exporting wool to America, as well as to France and Spain. After his father had died suddenly, John often spent his days and sometimes nights in Martin Maloney's house. Martin was the eldest of five children and John always enjoyed the time he spent with all of them. The export business thrived when his father was alive, but after his death, his mother, Kate, became a social butterfly and entertained lavishly, bringing friends, relatives and anyone who would come into her beautiful home. The parties often went on into the night and John would drift off to sleep to the strains of "Napper Tandy" and "Down by the Glenside".

It was during this time that Kate became friendly with a Conncmara fisherman – Colm O'Rourke, who lived in Salthill during the summer months with his sister Una. He came there every summer with three of his friends to fish for lobster. While Colm stayed with Una, his friends stayed further west in the little village of Spiddal which is nestled between the river and the sea. Colm was described as a 'fine figure of a man', dark and swarthy looking with powerful arms. He fished in the bay for the lobsters every day and, came back to stay with Una every evening.

One evening when they were having dinner together, Una looked across the table at her brother "any lobsters today?" she enquired

"Oh yes, I sold them all to the hotel near the bay. I should be able to sell to all the hotels around here".

"Hmm, that's good".

Already Una was thinking of her friend Kate and the invitation for Saturday evening.

"Would you like to come with me and visit Kate"?

"She's been on her own with her little boy for some time now".

"She'd like the company".

Before Colm could answer, Una said "keep those auld lobster pots out there in the outhouse and the fish smell as we go to see Kate". "She lives there near the Salmon Weir Bridge". Colm was silent. He knew that when Una decided to do something, it was pointless to argue.

—∞—

Colm and Kate were married three months after that Saturday evening meeting. They and John went to live in Innisbeg, while John's Uncle Patrick O'Dowd and his wife Celia took over the house and the failing business. John was seven years old when Páid was born two years later. Life was difficult but happy in their small cottage on the island of Innisbeg, but when Colm was drowned three years after that John was sent to live with Patrick and Celia, who were childless. There he stayed, went to school and learned about the export business from his uncle.

The dark clouds gathered. Suddenly the heavens opened and down came the rain, beating relentlessly against the car. John drove slowly along the twists and turns in the narrow road. The rain stopped just as suddenly as it had started, giving way to the rainbow and another rainbow – a double. He looked up at the sky – blue again, the clouds scattered towards the mountain in front of him. The colours of the rainbows were already fusing together. How could any artist capture the beauty and transience of this? John smiled – typical Connemara weather.

He turned a corner and there it was, standing stark against the sky – Martin and Honor's house. The Teachers Residence as it was called. It was an austere granite building with dormer windows and a rough path leading up to it, flanked on either side with whitewashed stones. At the sound of John's car Martin and Honor came out to meet him, embraced him warmly and led him towards the front door. "Showery weather again" Martin was saying.

Inside they walked straight into the sitting room. On the opposite wall was the staircase, leading to the bedrooms above. The sitting room was comfortably furnished with a large rug on the stone floor and two armchairs by the fire on the right hand wall. There was a dining table and chairs in the centre of the room and a small bookcase, filled with books set against the banisters. Honor disappeared into the kitchen on the left hand side and soon emerged with a tray of tea and sandwiches.

John and Martin were discussing the merits of the game of handball.

"I would like a game" Martin said.

"I don't play now as much as I used to".

John agreed.

"Yes, a game would be good".

"That's settled, so we can walk down to the ball alley after a while".

"Will you come with us, Honor? John asked.

"I would love to John, but I have some fresh mackerel I will be cooking while you are away."

"We'll look forward to that" Martin smiled at this wife.

Then, he hurriedly put two pairs of canvas shoes and a ball into a bag and they left the house, walking through the tree-lined road which led to the ball alley. It was deserted except for a few boys who were kicking a small ball around.

"What are you playing? John asked them.

"Or nothing, just kicking the ball around".

They sat nearby and watched John and Martin play a game of handball. After the game, the boys gathered around the two friends.

"Will you teach us how to play handball?" they asked excitedly.

"Sir", they looked at Martin.

"Will you teach us?"

Martin smiled, "Yes, I'll teach you".

The boys ran off, kicking the ball as they ran.

Martin was thinking of the boys. "Isn't it grand that they are so interested?" "I will get together with some of the lads who play sometimes and teach them."

"Every other house in the area has someone dying of consumption and the sanatoria are full". No wonder that those who can are leaving the country".

The sound of coughing in the classroom is deafening at times.

John thought of Páid and that rasping cough and a spear of pain ran through his heart.

Honor had just finished cooking the meal of fresh mackerel and new potatoes when Martin and John came through the door. "Just in time" Honor called from the kitchen – "the dinner is nearly ready". "We'll just change the shoes and have a wash", Martin called out, "won't be long". Honor served up the meal as they all sat at the table. "Had a good game?" She asked. "We played a few games" Martin told her, but I'm not as fit as I used to be".

"There were a few of the little boys up there and they were very interested in learning how to play the game. I promised I would teach them".

"This is a great meal, Honor". "You can't beat a fresh mackerel" John said.

"You know there's a Connemara man in New York by the name of Patrick J. McDonagh who won the World Championship and the New York Championship in handball a few years ago and won the gold medal in the Tailteann Games in Dublin".

Honor was smiling at John now.

"Well, it does our hearts good to hear that a man like that is doing so well in America, because, so many leave here to go over there and we never hear of them again, God help us!"

"That's true, John said – but that's not all, 'our champion was also captain of the Galway football team. An all round athlete, you might say".

"I'm thinking of going over there myself soon".

"Are you, John?" Martin and Honor cried in unison.

"Yes – my uncle wants me to go to New York and look after the business for a while".

Martin and Honor exchanged glances.

"Your uncle and Celia will miss you, as we all will".

Honor was clearing the table. Martin said quietly

"That's the way now".

John got up from the table stretched up to his full six feet.

"I'll be leaving now, it's a fair drive into Galway."

He looked sadly at his two friends.

"I'll come back and see you again before I leave for America".

"Make sure you do."

Honor embraced him as he walked towards the door. Outside, as he approached his car, they said their farewells. The sun was heading towards the sea and the corncrakes were singing their raucous songs in the fields. John drove back the same winding road towards Stonebridge, passed the harbour where the boats were moored. The sun was now sinking behind the little island of Innisbeg, as his heart was sinking at leaving poor Páid. "I will come back and see them all soon", he vowed as he drove in the direction of Oughterard and the little village of Moycullen, leaving behind the lonely, haunting and beautiful place that is Connemara.

He was just coming near Moycullen when he noticed that the car was running very low on petrol. "What an eejit I am", he thought – all that time playing and talking about handball and forgot to check the petrol gauge. He knew that there was a shop, which had a petrol pump outside not far away. He drove up right near the pump. A small man, wearing cannasna trousers, grey shirt and tweed cap came out and peered at John.

"Two gallons", John said.

"I'll do better than that Bejasus, I'll fill her up for you if you like".

The little man unscrewed the cap of the petrol tank.

"It's alright", John said "twos enough, I'm only going into town".

"Well I hope that'll be enough".

He pushed the lever hard to and fro on the pump, releasing two gallons through the hose.

"There you are, Sir – five bob".

He looked at John, smiling a toothless smile.

"Five bob"? John exclaimed, but before he could say anymore the little men went on –

"Ah no, I'm only codin', that'll be half a crown".

"Half a crown", John echoed.

"Now sir, you are lucky to be getting anything at all this evening and that's the right price, half a crown, on me oath, sir".

He looked steadily at John – removed his cap, ran his fingers through his greying thin hair and replaced the cap on to his head in a more comfortable position. John handed him a half crown piece and drove off.

"Why was it" John was thinking that everything had to be transacted with such a performance. It was the same at any of the cattle fairs. The fair in town that day was not far from his house and the street was packed, cattle, sheep owners and jobbers. The jobbers were distinctive by their dress. Smart suits were worn with the trousers tucked into the dung splattered wellington boots. The buying and selling of animals was a ritual – the owner asking for a certain amount of money and the jobber turning away in mock disbelief, coming back and offering half the price. The owner then turning away laughing mockingly and saying he would get a better price anywhere in the fair. So, the bantering went on all day and eventually the cattle were sold, both parties spitting on their hands and shaking on the deal.

John was coming near the town of Galway passing the familiar red brick houses and round by the old jail. He drove over the Salmon Weir Bridge and reached his house – a two storey house, overlooking the river. He parked the car, crossed the threshold and entered his home.

—~—

John was walking down the centre of New York City – a light spring in his step. He had not felt so light hearted for such a long time. The day was St. Patrick's Day. Why should he not celebrate? His uncle Joseph and Celia urged him to come here and see how the business was getting on and things were doing well. The economists were predicting great strides and the Stock Exchange was very active. The Theatres on Broadway were always packed. Radio networks had started. John wore The new fashion clothes.

So, he was happy. Life was good in New York City – very different to the life he left behind in Galway. His brother Páid had been taken ill with the consumption which had swept away so many. It was no different for Páid. "He lasted no time at all" someone told John at the wake. They buried Páid in the little graveyard by the sea. The friends and neighbours paid their respects to John. The boat was given to two of Páid's friends and John turned the key in the door of the little cottage and walked away. So many people on the island before him had walked away, leaving everything, most of whom would never return. John looked back at the cottage before he left the island. He was filled with grief and anger. He had a good mind to burn the place down – but no – that would not be right – there were the memories. Life in New York City eased the sorrow, so why then did he ache to go home? This ache pulling at him like the moon pulls at the sea.

The music from the ballroom was getting louder. He paid at the ticket office and went inside. The music and the atmosphere raised his spirits immediately. The Irish and New York voices intermingled. "Hi John" – he was greeted all round by various people from his neighbourhood. He walked along the crowded floor and found a place to stand at a column giving a view of the band. The dancing couples were dancing to the strain of "I'll be with you in Apple Blossom Time". Opposite him on the other side of the room there was a group of girls laughing and talking excitedly. He could catch a glimpse of them through the dancing couples. The music finished and the couples on the dance floor strayed across to their tables, giving John a better view of the girls. They were all shapes and sizes but John could not mistake the slim girl with the red gold hair. The band struck up the music again and the crowd sang "Here I go, singing low, bye bye blackbird". John crossed the floor in a few strides, stood opposite the red haired girl, saying "feet ok now?" Maura stared at the man standing before her. She looked up at him and saw his mischievous grin and laughing eyes.

"Yes" she faltered. He held his arms out to her and they swirled around to the music, being jostled by the crowd. John saw the beads of sweat on her forehead and her very flushed face. He picked her up in his arms and spun round and round, much to the delight of the applauding dancers. Maura was swept up in this excitement and all she could see was a sea of heads swimming before her. As the music and applause stopped John put her down gently and they walked towards the tables. Catching her breath, she looked at John who was now sitting opposite her. Many questions were forming in her mind. "Where did he come from this evening? Was he in New York long? She was amazed that he remembered her. But John was the one who asked the questions - "When did you arrive? Do you like New York?"

He looked at Maura's flushed face. Her shoulder length hair had given way to the fashionable bob with a hair slide fastened at the side. Her frail figure suited the dress she wore.

He remembered his dream - where he and Maura had been thrown together in Eóiniń Bán's cart on a lonely road in Connemara and at that thought the now familiar ache returned for a moment. He would go home, of course. He looked intensely at Maura. Would she return with him? Maura, in turn, looked at him. Suddenly, he was so serious. She wanted to know all about him.

In the weeks and months that followed Maura Mc Hugh and John O'Dowd spent a lot of time together. They explored New York City and spent many happy days at the beaches around the City, and so they decided to marry, returning home on the steamship President Polk.

The marriage ceremony took place in a church at Stonebridge with Martin and Honor standing as their witnesses. After the ceremony they headed back to Galway where Celia and a few neighbours were waiting. The large table which was in the centre of the lovely sitting room was laden with all the prepared food. The wedding cake was there with the small boxes arranged all around it into which pieces of cake would go and would be sent to friends and relatives who could not be present. Maura had always loved that room from the moment she had seen it, on that day when she visited Celia. It was a large room. As she walked in what struck Maura immediately was the tiled floor, of different colours, pink, white and yellow, and the large fireplace made of Connemara marble. On either side of the fireplace were the two inviting brown leather armchairs. On the side wall near the window was the floor to ceiling book case. The window was a sash window with the sill at least two feet in width. The house was several hundred years old and therefore had very thick walls.

Large cream lace curtains adorned the window and an old gramophone had been placed on the sill. Under the window was a leather chaise longue matching the armchairs, with a chenille wrap lying over the head and arm rests. On the back wall opposite the fireplace stood an upright piano with its yellowing keys and someone had said it could do with being tuned. The other side of the room was dominated by two windows identical to the one opposite which looked out on to the courtyard. These two were also adorned with lace curtains, having geranium plants in brass pots on the sills. Through these, there was a view of the river which flowed by at different speeds according to the seasons. The large table and eight chairs which was now in the centre of the room usually stood under these windows. The large expanse of wall was covered with family photographs as well as photographs taken of both Maura and John in New York and at the various beaches they had visited.

They lived happily with Celia in their house for a few years - going for long walks by the river, in all seasons. It was during one of these walks that Maura looked at John and said "our dream is coming true, John".

"Which dream is that?" John asked.

"Our baby, of course".

John could not hide the happiness in his eyes.

"A boy", John was laughing.

"Well, if that is so we'll name him John and if it turns out that we have a girl".

Maura stood and watched the river flowing by, "a girl, she'll be our dream, Aisling".

"You have it all figured out".

John was holding Maura's hand as they walked.

"We must tell Celia".

Celia was standing by the kitchen window looking out on to the garden. She was dressed in black and had done so ever since Joseph had passed on. Her hair was now white and she wore it combed tightly back into a bun at the nape of her neck. It was June. She loved the pink roses which were in bloom on the right hand side wall which ran along the entire length of the garden. They were the only flowers as the rest of the garden was given over to potatoes, cabbages, carrots and on the other side of the stone path were the lettuces, scallions and rhubarb, all of which she had sown in the Spring. She spent a lot of time tending and weeding and sometimes complained "my poor back is not able for this any more". She walked to the back door, taking a scissors and some newspaper with her. She came to the roses and cut a few blooms - mostly buds, and wrapped them in the piece of newspaper, dropped the scissors into her apron pocket and surveyed the rest of the garden.

"That rhubarb is growing wild", she muttered.

"Lovely day now, Ma'am" a man's voice shouted from down the end of the garden where the rhubarb was growing. Celia peered down and saw Mossie. Mossie shouted whether he was down at the end of the garden or standing beside you.

"Yes, indeed" Celia said "lovely now. Thank God."

"Great day Ma'am isn't it?" Mossie shouted.

"Yes, indeed" Celia shouted back.

Mossie jumped over the now broken down stone style and came and stood under the ash tree which was growing on the left hand side of the garden. "This is better", Celia was thinking, "I won't have to shout too much now". Mossie was a big man, overweight with a red face and bald - face redder than usual today because of the heat. He took out a handkerchief, which had seen better days, and mopped his brow, and sat down on the large rock under the tree. His old shirt and trousers were partially covered by the raincoat which was tied around the waist with a piece of twine. His shoes were down at heel and Mossie McGee never wore socks, summer or winter. He carried an old canvas bag around with him, handy for his various stuff - not least the odd salmon poached from the river. He would tramp through the woods nearby to his home. In the winter the only other piece of clothing he wore was a green jacket with brass buttons, giving rise to the rumour that he had retired from the army, fuel being added to that by the tune he sang, what seemed like a military type call - Da de Da, Da di Da, Da de Da, Da de Da, Da de Da. He was often heard before he was seen.

"You have a lovely garden there, Ma'am, fine looking cabbages".

"Yes" Celia agreed. "There's a great crop this year".

She handed Mossie a spade which was stuck in the clay.

"Here Mossie, dig up one of them to have with your dinner".

Mossie eagerly took the spade and dug up a large cabbage.

"Well, God bless you, Ma'am, there must be a place for you in heaven" he said as he was packing the cabbage into his bag.

"Not yet, I hope" Celia smiled.

"What happened to that pig you had last year" he asked.

"Oh, how I liked that pig" Celia remembered.

"He got out in the Spring, ran down the street all the way to the Square and caused such a commotion. A few of the lads down there, I believe, tried to catch him, but nothing has been heard of him since".

"Mmm, yes" Mossie said absentmindedly.

Celia had a feeling that Mossie knew more about the pig than he let on. He was walking towards the style.

"I'll be going now. I'll get a nice piece of bacon below in Ted's".

Ted's was a pub the other side of the woods where large pieces of bacon were sold as well as their homemade black pudding.

Celia left the garden and went into the house, holding the bunch of roses wrapped in the newspaper. She had picked them for Delia Daly, a neighbour who lived in the next street. Delia was a widow for many years and she entertained herself and half the street by playing the piano accordion and singing "God save Ireland cried the hero", among others. But now she was "very slack" according to her long suffering housekeeper, Mary Ann, whom Celia had talked to outside the Church after Mass one Sunday.

John and Maura were coming up the path chatting excitedly. Celia opened the door and Maura came through first.

"Oh Celia, we have such good news".

Celia put the flowers down on the hall table, "what on earth .....", before Celia could say any more,

"We are expecting the baby early next year", Maura blurted out and John stood in the background beaming.

"A baby in the house", Celia fought back the tears as she went over the hugged and kissed them both. She then picked up the flowers again.

"I'll put these in water".

John and Maura went into the sitting room and sat down at the table.

"Yes, a baby in the house", Maura whispered.

Celia came back with the roses in a vase and put it down on the table.

"There" she said, "beautiful roses for a beautiful baby".

She would cut some more roses for Delia tomorrow.

Delia's health deteriorated in the next few months and one night she passed away peacefully in her sleep, leaving a sad and lonely Mary Ann. Celia and John helped with the funeral arrangements and asked Mary Ann if she would like to come and live with them. She was very glad to do so, as she had been with Delia since she left the orphanage. Life was very different for her in the O'Dowd household. They asked her to stay on as their housekeeper. She accepted and as time went by she was very happy. Celia was very kind of her and as for Mr and Mrs O'Dowd, they were wonderful in Mary Ann's eyes.

"Herself" looking forward to the baby in a few months time. There was a great air of expectation in the home, even if Mrs O'Dowd had to rest such a lot during the day.

Maura gave birth to a baby girl shortly after going into the nursing home, but the birth left her very weak. The baby was healthy and beautiful, as Maura said. John watched anxiously, so proud of his baby girl yet fearful for Maura. As the days passed he hoped to see some recovery but Maura was becoming weaker day by day. The doctor told John that her heart had been weak for some years. John stayed with her every day. One evening he was called urgently. Maura was so weak, she could hardly speak. The priest was present giving her the Last Rites. When the priest left John went to her bedside and held her in his arms. Maura looked at John, smiled faintly and whispered "Aisling". He nodded. She closed her eyes, her spirit left her poor body and she lay peacefully in John's arms.

Aisling had an idyllic childhood. She was six days old when Celia and Mary Ann brought her home from the nursing home. The beautiful Maura was buried in the churchyard in Cashelmore - not far from the road when she and John had first met - just a few short years ago. In the years that followed John was often sombre, going out every day to look after his business - a business he had little appetite for at that time. Celia and MaryAnn saw his pain and supported him as best they could. Meanwhile, Aisling was a delightful child, popular with all her school friends and eager to join in any activity that was going on. She looked exactly like John, with thoughtful grey eyes and a shock of dark wavy hair. How he loved her and she him in return. They spent so much time together, going for long walks by the river when they could. Her birthday parties were great events for Aisling and her little friends. Celia, especially found great joy in looking after the little girl although her own health was failing. She looked to Mary Ann more and more for support and Mary Ann in return gave all her energy to the whole household. Aisling had great freedom playing with her friends within her home, climbing trees in the woods beyond, whipping tops up and down the street, which was devoid of traffic. They would play all kinds of games very often until twilight time when Celia would call out to her to come in as "the dew was falling". In the summertime Mary Ann would take Aisling and the friends down to the strand where they would bathe and learn to swim. They also learned how to pick cockles in the strand, prize them open and eat them there and then. They spent many hours picking brown and white edible seaweed. This seaweed was a great favourite with everyone. Adults came and filled up big bags which they would bring home - spread it all out in the sun to dry and store some away for the winter. The brown seaweed was eaten dry and tasted of the sea - very salty. The white seaweed was boiled with milk and was said to have very healthy properties - a nice hot drink and when it was allowed to cool, it set rather like a white blancmange and was eaten as a dessert.

"The mackerel are in" - the cry went up around August and people coming back from the seashore would say "They're throwing themselves up on the rocks". Locals and visitors alike were there with their spinner hooks and string fishing for the mackerel. The fish came in after shoals of sprats and when the tide went out they could be found in the rock pools choked by the sprats, hanging out of their mouths. This was an annual occurrence and people ate fresh mackerel for days. Some were busy, salting and smoking to store away for the winter months.

During the summer months also there was "Bonfire Night". Children would help the adults to gather turf for the fire by asking neighbours for a few sods or turf. The people all donated and by evening there was enough turf collected.

Old and young alike gathered around the bonfire. It was situated near the beach and all the fires could be seen in Co Clare, across the bay. No one seemed to know or care, at the time, why these fires were lit. Maybe it was a tradition handed down from Pagan times, some people thought.

In winter too, there were celebrations. Halloween was when children bobbed around trying to pick up apples in their teeth from a large tin bath of water, kneeling and keeping their hands behind their backs. After this very wet exercise, the next game was touching one of the four saucers laid out on the table. The saucers contained:

> Water – they would travel overseas
> Ring – get married
> Earth – death
> Religious object – enter a religious order

One of those was touched while blindfolded. Having touched one of them their destiny was sealed!

In the dark evenings of every St Stephens Day Aisling and her friends would gather in her house – burn some bottle corks in the fire, smear their faces with the burned corks, dress up in fanciful clothes and hats which were decorated with holly. The 'costumes' were borrowed from any adults who were willing and so the children became the mummers. They visited each house, were invited inside, whereupon they perform a dance. They would twirl round and round and interact with each other in a free fashion. After the dance, the people would try to recognise each one of them and there was great fun and laughter trying to do so – not always successfully. A small gift was always presented to them in the form of sweets or cakes. Leaving the houses, the colourful little troupe ran towards the convent, where they were invited in to perform their dance. The nuns would look closely at each of the mummers and usually recognised their pupils! They were then given their gifts – fruit seemed to be the preferred gift – apples from their orchard.

The traditional dances which were taught in school were very different from the free style of the mummers. They were very disciplined and the dancing teacher, who played the violin, marked out the floor with chalk while teaching the dances – the various reels, jigs and hornpipes. While these dances were performed at the end of term concert by the pupils – the teacher also performed some of the dances herself, while playing the violin as her accompaniment music, much to the great appreciation of her audience.

The formation dances were learned and performed at the Céilí, which were handed down through the generations. These Céilí were held mostly in Church halls and were attended by all the adults. The dances, such as the Sixteen-hand Reel, Walls of Limerick, The Bridge of Athlone and others were danced to music of the same name, played usually by a lone accordion player, relieved at various times in the evening by others who were proficient at playing the same instrument.

They were dances depicting old battles, perhaps reminiscent of the ancient Greek marching and military dances. The dances were also performed at the house dances, which were prevalent at the time (the word went round quickly as to where the house dance was held), but the larger formation dances were not performed due to lack of space.

Celia's health deteriorated and she passed away when Aisling was ten years old and so her care was left in Mary Ann's hands. John was becoming more and more morose and after a year he decided to sell the house and move back to New York. Realising that Aisling was too young to travel with him, it was decided with the new people in the house that Mary Ann and Aisling would remain there, Mary Ann continuing with her housekeeping duties as well as looking after Aisling. For Aisling's care, John would send a certain amount of money each month to both the new people and Mary Ann - an arrangement which worked well for a certain period of time. But gradually, Mary Ann came to the conclusion that this household was very different to living with John and Celia and it was not a proper environment for her and certainly not for Aisling.

Aisling was often awakened in the night by the loud arguments that went on by the drunken couple downstairs. Mary Ann wrote to John explaining the situation and reassuring him that she had talked to a middle-aged couple who would be glad to give Aisling a home, having no children of their own. She herself had known them for a long time. They were living in a small cottage in the village of Ard by the Sea. Besides, she had met a widower who had three young children and she agreed to marry him. John wrote back agreeing to her suggestion. So Aisling went to live with what Mary Ann called her new landlady and man. Landlady was kind and helped Aisling through her puberty even if she was irritable at times. Aisling missed her father and although he wrote to her regularly she wished she could be with him in New York, but he always said that she could join him when she was a little older.

One day after school, she was sitting at the kitchen table finishing her homework when Man came in, walked over to the table where she was sitting and touched her hair. Aisling shook her head and pushed his hand away.

She did not like Man. As she stood up from the table, packing her books into her bag, he stood close behind her and gripped her shoulders. Petrified, she broke free from his grasp, turned quickly around and kicked him in the shin as hard as she could. He bent over, holding his leg and through clenched teeth let out a string of oaths.

Aisling ran out of the house toward the sea, ran the entire length of the beach until she came to the rocks, where she sat down, out of breath. "What had she done? They would tell her father or maybe they wouldn't let her stay there any more." She stayed there sitting on a rock for a long time, getting wet with the sea spray frightened to go back, but knowing also that she had to go back. When she did return there was nobody about. She went to her room feeling the cold of the bare stone floor, and silently went to bed. She was awakened by a shuffling noise and a shadow coming towards her. What was that? She sat up in bed and screamed. The shadow and the shuffling noise disappeared. Aisling lay down again - praying that she would not see the shadow again. Then she heard the shrill voice of Landlady and the loud voice of Man arguing. The voices were so loud, yet she could not hear what they were saying. She covered her head with the sheet and went back to sleep.

Next morning she got up early and went to school without any breakfast. After school she came back, expecting to be confronted for kicking Man yesterday. But Landlady was sitting at the table saying:

"There you are Aisling, I'll get you something to eat, as you had no dinner yesterday."

Just then Man came in and limped towards the fire. He and Landlady glared at each other but nothing was said about that kick.

Shortly after that, Aisling wrote to John saying that she would like to go to the boarding school in town. Her friend Patsy was there already and she really liked it. John was very pleased that Aisling was happy to go to the boarding school and so he arranged it with the Nuns in charge that Aisling would start there that September.

Aisling thrived in the convent boarding school enjoying the company of her peers. She felt that one could express herself well in all her classes especially in the signing class, where her teacher quickly discovered that she had an exceptional singing voice. Singing was nothing new to Aisling. How often had she sung with Tommy Delaney who was her own age? When they were children at her parties they used to sing. He taught her 'Blackbird' and 'The Old House'. When visiting the homes of her friends she was always requested to sing around the fires. Tommy liked to sing outside at night, especially in the winter months. "If I were a blackbird I'd whistle and sing". She used to lie in bed, listening to him.

"Did you hear him again last night, Tommy the Street Singer? You would stand in the snow listening to him people would say".

But it didn't last. In a few years he didn't sing anymore.

"Why?" Aisling asked.

"His voice broke" someone said.

"But that shouldn't matter. He can still sing, can't he?"

"No, I don't think so".

Aisling was puzzled and saddened to hear this. Her own voice was nurtured and encouraged. She had singing lessons. She sang solo for visiting dignitaries at the convent. She was put forward as part of a group and sang in the Church Choir, from the Mesa Cantata to the Palestrina.

Patsy Quinn was Aisling's friend. She was two years older than Aisling and did not seem to have many friends. She had straight short black hair and a trim figure and seemed to run everywhere rather than walk. She did not seem to have many friends, maybe because she was sometimes gruff and domineering. She was an only child herself and seemed protective towards Aisling.

Aisling spent many of the school holidays in the convent and often felt lonely when she saw all the other girls going home. Patsy realised this and asked Aisling if she would like to stay with herself, her mother and Aunt Lily when holiday time came around. Delighted with this invitation Patsy told John in her letter to him all about it. John wrote thanking Patsy's mother and told Aisling once again that she would join him in New York when she was more mature. This settled, Aisling met Patsy's family.

Patsy's home was a tall three storey building not far from the convent. It was in a street with similar buildings on either side. There was a large haberdashery shop on one corner and a small pub on the other corner. The Quinns had lived there for many years. Mary, Patsy's mother, had married Tom Quinn, who had inherited the home from his parents and Patsy was born there. Tom also inherited their thriving business. They had been prudent in their financial dealings and lived frugally, and had always hoped that one day Tom would follow in their footsteps and continue to run the business. They had a small shop in the next street which proudly displayed a modest sign over the door - 'Patrick Quinn - Cobbler'.

Inside the shop there was a strong smell of leather and where Patrick, wearing his apron worked at his bench by the window, with his last, nails, hammers and large pieces of leather from which he cut what he needed for his boot and shoe mending. As well as that he had on display for sale, various types of footwear - from sturdy hob nailed boots and Wellingtons to children's canvas shoes. On the wall where he worked were shelves filled with tins of polish and brushes. People came into chat to Patrick and ask him to stretch their shoes for them, having bought them a size too small. Women seemed to have been in the majority here! Patrick, as always, obliged by putting the shoe stretcher into the shoes and advice was offered by people waiting to collect their footwear. "Stuff wet newspapers into them overnight - that might help".

But Tom was not interested in the business. He was a gambler. He sold the business, telling Mary that he had debts to pay. Mary was dismayed - not knowing that the handsome debonair man she married had accumulated so much debt.

"No more debts now" he assured her as he got a job as a manager in one of the hotels in Salthill, and with the arrival of their baby they would have happy times and happy times they had indeed when Patsy arrived. Short lived. He soon announced that he landed a job in one of London's prestigious West End hotels and there would be ample money in the future and he would come home as often as possible. True to his word, he did exactly that but soon the money began to dwindle and the homecomings were less frequent.

By the time Patsy was one year old, Mary had not seen or heard from him in many months. By his rugged good looks and undoubted charm he became involved with one of the many aristocratic English families, much of whose money he gambled and lost. It was rumoured that the last time he was seen it was on board ship bound for Australia, going to Ballarat in search of gold. Among the many stories regarding his disappearance was the one that he and the heiress of the family whose money he had lost had gone to her relatives in the Argentine.

So, Mary was left almost destitute. It was at this time that Lily O'Grady, her sister, came to stay. She had heard of Mary's misfortune while she was working in Dublin, as a civil servant, from Eileen O'Donnell, Mary's former next door neighbour as well as letters received from Mary. She arrived by train at Mary's house, dropped her suitcase in the hall (the front door always left open) and announced that she had given up her job in Dublin and was going to stay with Mary and the baby, Patsy, complaining bitterly about Tom Quinn's conduct.

Lily was small in stature, with a mass of fair wavy hair, bird-like features and eyes which were always enquiring and suspicious. She wore the latest fashionable clothes and shoes of very high heels, clicking about outdoors and indoors, throwing them off only when she went up the stairs, of which there were many. Mary was grateful to Lily if a little in awe. She had the same fair hair as Lily, but that's where the resemblance ended. Mary was tall, with a quick smile and patient. They discussed their future in the house and decided that it was big enough to be used as a guest house for three or four people. Josie O'Kane, a taxi driver, who was very disappointed with his current 'digs' was their first guest. Then, there were the commercial travellers who came and went at regular intervals. Patsy grew up in a happy home with her mother and Aunt Lily, Mary doing the household chores while Lily did the decorating and oversaw the finances – having time to join the Amateur Dramatic Society.

The house was tall and narrow, having two rooms off the hall, the dining room, leading directly into the kitchen with the back door opening onto the yard. On the first floor was the sitting room towards the front of the house with two bedrooms on that floor and the bathroom and two other bedrooms on the top floor.

This was the house in which Aisling would be spending her holiday time. Patsy helped her carry her luggage – a few clothes and mainly books from the school.

It was Sunday and the dining room table was set for the evening meal. Aisling sat opposite Patsy who introduced her to Mrs Quinn – Patsy's mother. Aunt Lily and Josie O'Kane, the taxi driver who had been staying there for many years now, sat opposite each other. Josie was small, rotund and red faced. He spoke very little, especially during meal times. He looked at Aisling, smiled amiably and nodded. "Usually we have other people staying but they are away for the weekend" Patsy told her.

After the meal was finished Mary showed Aisling to her room, which she would share with Patsy. It was situated on the first floor, two beds, wardrobe and dressing table with pink eiderdowns on the beds.

"The walls are nice" Aisling remarked.

"Oh, Lily does all the decorating" Mary was saying, "pink distemper and she paints on the roses".

"It looks just like wallpaper" Aisling said.

"It does" – Mary was very proud of Lily.

"She did the sitting room last year as well. She is very artistic."

So it was that Aisling shared Patsy's home during the school holidays. They played and swam in Salthill during the summer and helped Lily in the Amateur Dramatics at other times. They spent many happy times together during the next few years. One year before Aisling was due to leave school, Patsy became dissatisfied with everything and she wanted to see more of the world, so she made her decision.

They both walked from Taylor's Hill into the centre of town – just for the walk. Patsy wanted to tell Aisling of her decision not to return to school that September – that she wanted to go to London to her uncle's family and start work.

"What work will you do?" Aisling was taken aback.

"I don't know yet", Patsy shrugged.

"Does your Mother and Aunt Lily know?"

"No".

Suddenly, Patsy grabbed Aisling's arm.

"Don't look at him", referring to the man walking towards them.

"Look straight ahead".

"Who?"

Aisling was pulled along.

"Him – don't look".

"Why not?"

Patsy pulled at Aisling's arm,

"Come on, walk quicker .... Don't ....".

"Well, helloooo, les girls!"

He smiled at the two girls, showing a gold tooth. He was about the same height as Patsy it seemed to Aisling, with dark hair, sleeked back with Brilliantine, dark eyes which darted back and forth between the two, wearing a light grey suit, tan waistcoat, white shirt and yellow bowtie. He was very thin and he walked towards them in a cat-like gait in his brown suede shoes.

“Are you well?” looking at Patsy.

Without waiting for a reply he asked

“And how is your Aunt Lily?” in a slow deliberate voice.

“She’s well, thank you”.

“Good” he said, “très bon”.

“Well, I’m a busy man. I’ll be on my way. Au Revoir”.

He bowed before the two girls.

“Who is he?” Aisling was intrigued, “And why did he bow like he was on the stage?”

“Cos he’s an eegit”, Patsy laughed, “And all that speaking French. They are the only few words he knows. He told Aunt Lily that he was in the French Foreign Legion.”

“Really”, Aisling was still intrigued.

“What does Aunt Lily say?”

“He never saw the French Foreign Legion”, Patsy said matter-of-factly.

"Aunt Lily said 'May God forgive him for telling lies, the Spalpeen – and don't trust any man who wears suede shoes."

"Why", Aisling wondered.

"I dunno" Patsy was walking quickly, "let's go and have coffee at the Rimini Café. It's nice in there. They serve lovely ice cream as well."

The Rimini Café was cheerfully decorated, having pastel colour square table tops to accommodate four people. The two friends chose a table by the window and sat down. The waitress came over and they ordered two coffees.

"You'll never guess who's over there by the counter" Aisling said.

"It's Mikey and Liam. They're getting ready to leave."

Mikey also spotted them and they came walking over.

"Hello, we haven't met for ages. What are you doing now?"

"Nothing much", Aisling was interested.

"What are you doing?" Mikey looked at Aisling, she had grown up a lot, he thought.

"We are both going to the Jez – going back in September".

"Yes, I'm going back in September also."

"Well, I won't be going back", Patsy said, "better things to do".

"And what would that be?" Liam asked.

The waitress came with the two coffees.

"Well", Mikey said "we'll be off.

By the way, what are you doing on Sunday?"

"Why?" Aisling asked.

"Because" Mikey said deliberately, "the two of us and my sister, you remember her don't you, are going on the boat to the Aran Islands. Why don't you come with us?"

Aisling and Patsy looked at each other.

"Well" Patsy said nonchalantly, "we might. We'll have to find out at home. We can meet here tomorrow and let you know."

"All right so", Mikey said, "tomorrow" and headed towards the door.

Aisling and Patsy looked excitedly at each other.

"Aran Islands on the boat, I'd love to go, would you Patsy?"

Aisling was thinking of Mikey and how handsome he looked.

"Yes", Patsy was looking at her coffee.

"We'll have to go somehow. Why is this coffee so hot? I'll ask for more milk."

"No, don't", Aisling put the spoon into her cup.

"Go on, put the spoon in to the cup, that will cool it down".

"How will that cool it down?" Patsy was getting impatient.

"Something to do with the metal in the spoon" Aisling said smiling at Patsy.

Patsy put the spoon into the coffee and left it for a minute or so.

"Well, I'm going to drink it now", Patsy sipped the coffee.

"Oh, yes, it's alright".

They finished the coffee and Aisling paid the sixpence to the waitress who then went away.

"We'll have to leave a tip."

Aisling was looking in her purse, "but I don't think I have enough. What have you got?"

Patsy looked in her purse.

“I only have a threepenny bit and tuppence ha’penny”.

“That threepenny bit will do”, Aisling told her.

“I can’t leave that – I’m saving them until I have ten or so, but I’ll leave the tuppence ha’penny.”

They left the café and walked along the street, stopping now and then to look at the clothes shop windows.

“Why do you want to save the threepenny bits?”

“Because, because” Patsy said teasingly.

“Go on, tell me”.

“I’m going to make a bracelet out of them”.

“How?”

Aisling knew that Patsy had some strange ideas at times. They both stopped together and stared at the vision in the shop window. One mannequin standing alone, wearing a yellow and white dress with a full skirt, reaching down to the mid calf.

“Wouldn’t we love to wear that on the boat on Sunday” Aisling said dreamily.

They walked on, “but tell me about the bracelet”.

"Well, you know Eileen next door – she came home from Dublin not long ago, when you were back in the convent. Did you ever meet her"

"I did once I think" Aisling said.

"She doesn't often come home" Patsy continued.

"She's a friend of Aunt Lily's and they were in the sitting room getting ready to go out somewhere. Oh, Aisling, she looked like a film star, her red hair piled on top of her head, and a beautiful frock down to the middle of her legs, the New Look she called it, like that one we first saw in the window – high heels the same as Aunt Lily wears. She put on bright red lipstick and had red nails to match".

She paused and took a deep breath.

"She is so tall and slim. She would make two of Aunt Lily."

The two girls giggled.

"She was smoking a cigarette through a cigarette holder. Aunt Lily was admiring the holder so Eileen took one out of her bag and gave it to her".

"Did Aunt Lily use it?"

"Oh, yes" Patsy went on, "she said she was going to get one as her fingers were becoming brown with the smoke. That's when I saw the bracelet Eileen wore – made of threepenny bits. So I went down to the kitchen, made them some tea and brought it up on a tray with some biscuits. I put the tray on the table and they were talking and laughing and I heard the name Pièrre."

"Who – who's this Pièrre?"

"You know Aisling, that fella we met today who spoke in French. He calls himself Pierre because he helps out at the Amateur Dramatics. My mother says that his name is Jack De Vere and he works down in the docks."

"Why did he change his name I wonder", Aisling wanted to know.

"He says it's his stage name – a lot of people change their names. My name is Patricia you know – not Patsy."

They were nearly home now and they remembered that they had to have permission to go to the Aran Islands on Sunday with Mikey Doyle and his cousin Liam . Mary was upstairs in the sitting room doing her knitting and listening to the wireless. She heard the girls come in and she turned the volume down. They came in and sat down on the sofa opposite Mary.

"Well, who did you see around the town?" Mary asked as she continued with her knitting.

"Oh, a few people – Pièrre for one. He was asking for Aunt Lily".

"Oh yes", Mary did not look up from her knitting.

"Anyone else?"

"Well, yes" – Patsy was hesitant.

The two girls looked at each other. Mary put her knitting down and looked keenly from one to the other.

"You know Mikey Doyle", Aisling wanted to tell the story.

"We met him and his cousin Liam in the Rimini Café".

She finished the story by saying that they would like to go to the Aran Islands with them on Sunday and they had told the boys that they would let them know tomorrow. Mary knew both families.

"That Mikey is such a lovely boy. I see him at Mass on Sunday, nearly always with the family, but sometimes with his sister Sheila."

She leaned towards Aisling and lowered her voice.

"She's not right, you know, the poor creature, God bless the mark, the other boy is their cousin."

Mary sat comfortably in her chair again.

"They are all very friendly now, but it wasn't always like that".

Patsy stood up, looked at Aisling quickly, rolled her eyes to heaven and said

"I'll go and make some tea".

"Oh yes, do" Mary said, "Lily will be home soon, she's just gone to the dramatics and then we can have something to eat".

"As I was saying", she looked at Aisling who was listening intently.

Mary knew that she had an appreciative audience as Aisling was always interested in families. This time it was about the Doyle family and she wanted to know everything.

Patsy came back, put the tray of three cups of tea on the table and handed one to Mary,

"Here you are Mum".

She bent over and kissed her mother's cheek.

"Have you finished telling Aisling about the Doyles and their feud?"

Patsy and her mother smiled at each other and Aisling observed the great tenderness between them.

Mary sipped her tea.

"This is a lovely cup of tea Patsy – just right – not too much sugar. I think you two will be in very good company on Sunday with the Doyle boys and Sheila. You'll have to wear warm clothes. It gets cold on that boat going over. Its a few hours journey and sometimes the bay can be choppy."

The girls did not care about the weather – being cold or anything else. They were going to the Aran Islands on Sunday. They got up and danced around the room laughing and shrieking.

"What's all the noise?" Lily appeared at the sitting room door.

"Oh, they're going to Aran on Sunday with the Doyle boys" Mary shouted above the din.

"Girls, girls, calm down and tell me".

She was putting a cigarette into the holder. She walked over to Mary,

"Are you sure they'll be alright? I don't know if Pièrre will be there on Sunday."

"Pièrre what" – Patsy started to ask.

"Pièrre", Mary said patiently, "as he calls himself now, is Jack and he works on the boat that goes in and out of the Aran Islands."

"Pièrre who is Jack, who worked on the boat, and does he say Au Revoir to the passengers when they leave?" Patsy asked mockingly.

The two girls sat on the sofa again and laughed uncontrollably.

"Now – that's enough".

Lily drew hard on her cigarette, got up from her seat and went to the mirror adjusting her hair and peering at her eye make-up.

"It's lovely over there on a fine day – nice little beaches. Maybe we'll go ourselves, should we, Mary?"

Patsy and Aisling were suddenly quiet. Mary remembered her one and only trip over there. She and Tom were not long married when they decided to go over for the day. It was then that they met Jack de Vere who was very attentive to Mary while she suffered sea sickness all the way there and back. No, she would not go again.

"No, I won't be going on Sunday", she said.

"Maybe another time".

"Yes," Lily agreed, "maybe another time."

She winked at Mary. Patsy and Aisling had to stifle the sighs of relief.

The boys were waiting for them at the Rimini Café and they immediately knew that the girls would be joining them on Sunday, judging by their smiles.

On Sunday morning, the five friends, Aisling O'Dowd, Patsy Quinn, Mikey, Liam and Sheila Doyle boarded the steamer, sailing through the bay, going to Innismore, the largest of the Aran Islands. It was a glorious summer's day – no sign of any rough sea which Mary had feared and a soft breeze blew in from the islands. Soon the steamer reached Kilronan Harbour and they all stepped ashore. They had decided while on the boat that they would visit Dun Angus, an Iron Age fort on the other side of the island. The mode of transport they would use would be a horse and sidecar and before that they sat outside the pub which was nearby. Two fishermen passed them on their way into the pub.

They greeted the friends who looked at each other in surprise.

"I know that all Irish is spoken on these islands but I didn't know that they spoke Spanish as well".

Aisling turned to Mikey.

"No, they don't speak Spanish as well", Mikey told her with a smile.

"They are fishermen who come up here from Spain quite often and they stay in the pub."

"Come on".

Patsy was anxious to go.

"Will you boys carry these bags? There's some picnic food in them that my mother packed".

"Oh, we have some picnic food as well", Sheila said timidly.

They paid the man waiting with the horse and sidecar. The girls sat on one side with Sheila in the middle and the boys sat on the other side, so they were seated back to back. It was a pleasant journey, travelling the steep hills and dales in the road. Finally, they reached the Dun Angus fort.

They marvelled at the ancient semi-circular monument perched high on the cliff. Who built this and why? It looks like maybe to keep the enemy out. They walked around in awe, full of questions.

"Who built it and why seems to be unknown" Mikey offered.

"The Spanish men who come here for the fishing say that they have structures like this in Spain, which were built in what they called the Celtic Era in Spain."

The others stood and stared at Mikey. Patsy was sceptical,

"How do you know all this, Mikey?"

"Well, because ....".

They all laughed when Sheila interrupted "because Mikey knows everything".

They sat down by the cliffs to enjoy the picnic, looking across the bay at the even bigger cliffs of Moher. They threw their last crumbs to the waiting seagulls which were swooping and squawking around them and ran down the hill to the waiting sidecar. They returned to the harbour where the steamer was due to sail later that evening.

They all sat on deck as the boat sailed through the calm water and it was twilight time when they left the shore. When darkness had fallen they watched the falling stars criss cross the sky and ending in the horizon – much to their delight. Sheila, who was sitting next to Mikey especially enjoyed the spectacle, saying

"Look Mikey, they are souls going to heaven, aren't they?"

"You could well be right Sheila".

Aisling looked at Mikey and saw how thoughtful he was, even distant at times.

Saying their goodbyes as they left the steamer, Mikey whispered to Aisling "See you tomorrow". Lying in their beds that night, Aisling was not sleepy.

"Didn't we have a lovely day Patsy?"

"Yes, that boat reminded me of the one I'll be going on when I go to London, but I haven't told my mother yet. I'll tell her tomorrow."

"Yes, you should" Aisling murmured.

"Isn't Mikey the image of Alan Ladd?"

Patsy turned on her side and looked at Aisling,

“He is not” she said slowly and laughed.

“He is! He is!”

Aisling was dreaming of seeing him tomorrow.

“Oh well – beauty is in the eye of the beholder – as my mother would say. Goodnight and sweet dreams.”

Having walked and talked along the riverbank Aisling and Mikey sat down under an old oak tree, which was surrounded by crab apple tress, rocks covered in moss, clumps of nettles here and there and grass which was overgrown. They sat close together.

“So, you would like to take up signing as a career”, Mikey said, scraping some mud off his shoes with a twig.

“I would”.

My music teacher is getting in touch with my father about it”.

Aisling sat with her back against the tree trunk, looking up into the branches and listening to the birds.

“Listen to that bird, Mikey. That’s a thrush and that one over there in the higher branch is a blackbird. The blackbird is so pure and distinctive. I love listening to them, do you?”

“No, I can’t say I listen to them that intently”.

Mikey was looking up into the tree. Aisling looked quickly at his profile.

"Mikey, you look just like Alan Ladd".

"What Aisling, what are you saying – Alan Ladd indeed."

Suddenly he leaned over and kissed her. Aisling felt his lips on hers and the rim of his glasses touched her cheek. Mikey sat upright again and looked up into the tree remaining silent.

"Well, Mikey Doyle, if you can kiss me, I can kiss you as well."

She leaned forward but as she lurched towards him, he lost his balance and rolled down towards the nettles, losing his glasses.

"Oh Mikey, I'm sorry".

Aisling got up, but already Mikey was face down among the nettles. She found the glasses and handed them to him. He was now standing and brushing himself down of all the foliage he had on his clothes. His face was red and blotchy. Collecting a few dock leaves, Aisling spat on some and gave a few to Mikey, saying

"Here, spit on these and stick them to you face", which he did as well as sticking the ones that Aisling had spat on. When his face was covered with the leaves they headed for home. Aisling thought momentarily that he looked comical, but was more concerned about his face being burned. At the edge of the wood Mikey removed the leaves.

"Any better now?" Aisling asked.

"I'm alright, your spit must have healing properties".

He looked at Aisling with a wry smile. They each said their goodbyes and went their separate ways towards home.

That night Aisling told Patsy what happened to Mikey's face. She laughed uproariously saying

"I bet he doesn't look like Alan Ladd now".

"Ah, don't laugh, Patsy, his face was nearly all burned. I hope he'll be alright".

"Of course he will, it's only a nettle sting."

Patsy was suddenly very quiet.

"I told Mum that I wanted to go to London to my Uncle. She wasn't very happy but after a long conversation she said she would write to her brother, Brian, and arrange for me to stay with them. I might find out something about my father because Mum or Aunt Lily never mention him. Surely, my Uncle Brian would know something. All I know about him is that he went abroad years ago. Aisling, I don't know where he is – he could be dead for all I know. Oh, my poor father".

Patsy slumped on to the sofa and sobbed uncontrollably. Aisling hated to see her friend so unhappy. She went to the bathroom, brought back a towel, gave it to Patsy, saying

"Please don't cry, wipe your eyes".

Patsy sat up, took the towel, wiped her eyes, blew her nose.

"Thanks Aisling."

"Your Uncle is bound to know where your father is, and maybe Aunt Lily knows more than you think. You won't know unless you ask. Do ask her tomorrow."

"I will."

It was Christmas in the convent and all the girls had gone home, leaving Aisling alone. Patsy had gone to London and she had not heard from Mikey. She felt more desolate than ever. No, she could not stay here. She longed to see her father and she wanted to start her singing career.

Aisling stepped ashore at New York harbour having spent four days at sea out of Cobm, Co Cork. The voyage was pleasant but she was glad to have arrived safely as she was full of enthusiasm for seeing her father again after such a long time and also to see part of the New World. She felt herself to be part of history, making the same journey as the millions who had come here before her. She knew that she was fortunate, having her father to greet her, unlike her forebears, most of whom had no one, had nothing – only their courage.

There he stood, her father, waiting, looking elegant as always. He looked the same as she had remembered him. He had not changed one bit, Aisling thought as she ran to embrace him. The luggage was packed into the waiting taxi and they sped towards the centre of the City.

"So this is New York"

she said, looked out the window at the very tall buildings but could not see the top of the skyscrapers from inside the taxi. John, meanwhile drunk in the beauty of his daughter feeling proud and happy, and he delighted in her sheer lust for life. They reached their apartment near to Central Park and as they left the elevator they could hear the strains of a male voice singing the scales. Aisling smiled and looked enquiringly at John.

"Oh, that's Mario from the apartment above. He sings in the Opera. He and his mother live there. You will probably meet them tomorrow".

They entered John's large apartment and Aisling went straight over to the living room window. Looking out she saw the skyscrapers all around and some of the trees of the Park in the distance.

"It's like living with the birds, isn't it John?"

She looked shyly at John. Should she call him John or Dad? It was so long since she had called him

Dad – always Dear Dad in her letters from school – all of which were always censored as were his letters to her. Somehow she felt more comfortable saying "John" and he did not seem to mind as he made no comment about it.

Next morning they were up early. They had decided the night before to visit the warehouse and office. Just as they were getting ready to leave there was a knock at the door. John answered it.

"Good morning Carla, we were just leaving but come in. Aisling, this is Carla Del Amica from the apartment upstairs."

Carla crossed over to Aisling and enveloped her in a warm embrace.

"So, you are Aisling. Oh! You look just like your father."

"Thank you Mrs Del Amica".

"Call me Carla. I see you are going to business with your father, but you must come to dinner with Mario and myself this evening."

"That's very kind", John said.

"We would be delighted, wouldn't we Aisling?"

Aisling nodded and smiled. They left the apartment building and stepped into the street to the roar of the New York traffic. John hailed a cab and soon they were entering a large warehouse down by the wharf. Inside there was more noise – this time the heavy machines which were transporting bales of wool to the waiting trucks. They climbed the stairs to what Aisling thought was another apartment but was, in fact, an office suite. They stepped into the outer office.

"Good morning, Jessie"

John cheerily greeted the young woman sitting at the desk, and nodded to the young man who was sitting on the side of the desk and smoking a cigarette.

"Let me introduce you to Aisling, my daughter. Aisling, this is my secretary, Jessie."

Jessie stood up. She smiled warmly at Aisling and they shook hands.

"This is my brother, Max."

Max did not move from where he was sitting. He gave Aisling an uninterested look and said "Yea, hi." John and Aisling moved on into John's office.

"You really should have stood up, Maxi, when John introduced his daughter", Jessie reprimanded her brother.

"Yea, ok, Sis, I'll be off. Thanks for the dough."

Max unravelled his lithe body from the desk and sauntered towards the door.

Jessica and Max Wainwright were twins. They were the children of Bill and Alice Wainwright who were old friends of John O'Dowd. They had met John when he studied in Dublin for a brief period of time. They had talked then of going to America, California, they said, out to the sun, they said, but mostly to entertain. Alice was the singer in a band and Bill played the piano. So, they left Dublin and went to California and joined a band which played in one of the many ballrooms. Shortly after their arrival their twins were born.

Alice was dubbed "The girl with the golden voice" and Bill became "the keyboard man". The ballroom was crowded every night and there was applause of great appreciation for the band members after each dance, applause being the loudest for Alice and Bill. They lived in Los Angeles enjoying their new found fame and fortune. Although there were overjoyed by the birth of their twins, they both realised that Alice would not be working quite as much as before. They had agreed upon this before the birth. Bill, of course, continued to play the piano. However, they had not anticipated how the girl with "the golden voice" would be missed from the ballroom. People sent messages and many requests to Bill, asking for Alice to return only after a few months absence and Alice herself found it difficult not to appear on stage again. So, it was decided that the children would be placed in the care of a children's nurse and Alice returned to her beloved singing career. But the euphoria was short lived. The children did not seem to be thriving and Bill felt, more and more, that they should be cared for by their mother, keeping the nanny to help when needed. Bill was exaggerating – Alice was sure of it. The children were perfectly happy with the nanny and she steadfastly refused to see Bill's point of view. Her golden voice and her spirit soared as she sang to the thunderous applause. Bill played but became dejected. His beautiful children, what would become of them, their twins, Jessica and Max. After a few months had passed, Alice hardly ever seemed to see them anymore. She was exhausted after each performance. What was happening to them? Bill became determined this would not continue. They had not travelled from Dublin, all that way across America, worked so hard these last few years, settled in their lovely home by the ocean, had made friends, to see it all go wrong. He would talk to Alice.

"Stay at home and not sing – are you mad?"

Alice stormed around the living room. Bill was patient.

"Alice, you must see that the crowds are diminishing. The ballrooms are not what they used to be when we first started here."

"Now I know you're mad" Alice retorted.

"Did you hear the applause for me last night and every other night?"

Bill looked at her sadly. Did she really not realise that things were changing. The glory days were changing for the dance places. They would move to Chicago where he would find work at a piano bar or at one of the many night clubs.

"What about Chicago, Alice? It is the place for piano bars and ..."

"Chicago", Alice screamed.

She bent over and laughed loudly, mockingly.

"You go to Chicago. I am not leaving my beautiful home in the sun."

The door bell rang. Bill went to the hall and opened the front door. Gus Toner, the trumpet player, was standing on the door step. Bill looked at his pale face and dishevelled hair.

"What's wrong?"

Gus walked past Bill into the living room.

"We're finished".

He looked across from Bill to Alice.

"Haven't you heard? The ballroom was burned down early hours of this morning."

He stood five feet six in his stocky frame, his usual happy self transformed into the picture of gloom.

Alice shrieked and fell on to the sofa. Her ballroom on fire – no – not the dance floor, the chandeliers, her upholstered furniture, her castle with its domed turrets, her palace.

"My own castle" she whispered.

She lay face down on the sofa and cried loudly and uncontrollably. Suddenly she jumped up, wiping her face with her sleeves and glared at Bill and Gus.

"So, that's it, anything to stop me singing. How could you stoop so low as to burn down the ballroom?"

Both men stared at her.

"Alice, Alice", Bill walked over to her.

"Neither Gus nor I had anything to do with the fire."

"Of course we didn't", Gus faltered. He thought she must be in shock.

"I just came by to tell you that the band is meeting at my place this evening".

He walked to the front door.

"You will come, won't you?" Bill followed him.

"We'll be there, Gus."

Bill and Alice sat at the dining room table.

"Alice, I know you've had a shock, well, we all have, but we must get to that meeting this evening."

Alice was silent for a long time. After much cajoling Bill persuaded her to go with him to the meeting, where she sat aloof and unimpressed with the proceedings. But, she recovered sufficiently later, seeing everyone's distress at what had happened, to be able to talk about it, and was grateful that no one had been hurt. She heard snippets of conversation as she moved about.

"It's not the first time a ballroom has been burned, you know."

"Yes –things are changing around here."

"Jazz is the latest thing, I hear."

Gus found Alice.

"Alice, come on, someone I want you to meet."

She looked contritely at him.

"Gus, about this morning."

"Forget it, Alice, everyone is in such a state of shock."

Sitting at a table in the far corner of the room was Bill, talking to a man that Alice did not recognise. They stood up as Alice and Gus approached. The introductions over, they all sat at the table.

"As I was saying to Bill", Benny Lomax, the music promoter, was looking straight at Alice. "Chicago really is the place to be now. All the jazz stars are there. I see them all. You could be a jazz singer."

Alice stared at Lomax.

“I could be a jazz singer?”

Lomax’s large frame sat uncomfortably in his chair, his bejewelled hand holding his glass, beads of sweat glistening on his balding hairline, answered.

“But, of course, with your tones, my dear”, his voice trailed away.

He looked away from Alice to the two men.

“Am I right? Of course I am. Have we a deal? Who’s coming to Chicago?”

“Benny” Bill said, “It’s a good offer, but we must talk things over.” Benny Lomax got up.

“Ok, make it soon. See you tomorrow.”

Alice’s spirits had improved considerably on their return home.

“A jazz singer, Bill, me!”

“Yes, Alice, and me a piano player in a jazz band. I think the children will love it, especially Max, who is doing so well with the trumpet.”

“Maybe a chance to meet my idols”, Alice went on dreamily. Ella Fitzgerald and Billie Halliday.”

Bill was relieved that Alice was happy to leave the West Coast.

"Gus will be coming with us to play in Chicago. He doesn't want to miss out on the tuition for Max, 'My Protégé' he calls him."

"Mm, ok", Alice mumbled.

Bill, his twins, Jessica and Max and Gus arrived in New York having spent several years in Chicago. Difficult years. Alice had not become a jazz singer, as she had dreamed. Bill and Gus played in a jazz band. Jessica was very studious and did well at school and Max became very proficient at playing the trumpet under Gus's tuition. Alice accompanied Bill and Gus to the nightclub and often stayed on long after the band stopped playing, drinking and dancing to the early hours. Sometimes she would not return home at all for days on end. Bill was in despair almost, when one day she told him she was leaving the family home and going to stay with a friend, so she packed her bags and left. Bill decided then to travel to New York, having contacted his old friend John O'Dowd. Jessica became John's secretary and the three men played in one of New York's new clubs. By the time Aisling arrived, Max was well known in the band, Maxi Wainwright on trumpet. Jessica learned about John's business and was a true and faithful friend.

John sat at the large desk in the inner office.

"This is where I've been doing all my work while you were in the school", he told Aisling.

She looked around at the sparsely furnished and slightly shabby room. The large desk and two leather chairs were well worn with age, the carpet threadbare, the wallpaper, typical of the style of the twenties, was now peeling in places. The two large windows allowed in the sunlight which only served to show up the film of dust on the ledges and on John's pictures of his sporting heroes. She had not expected this, but what had she expected? Nothing. She had not thought about it. But now, she would think about it. She looked at John. He needed her now. She would improve the look of this office and learn all about the business.

That evening John and Aisling visited Carla and Mario as planned. After the meal, Mario played the piano, which was situated in the corner of the sitting room. Mario and Aisling sat together and Aisling sang 'Panis Angelius' in her soprano voice. "You must come to the Opera with me" Mario said.

Next morning Aisling went to the workplace as usual and told Jessie about the invitation to the Opera, but also confessed that now she knew what homesickness meant. She missed the company of her friends at the school, people her own age.

"I really haven't met any young people here, except yourself and Max, of course.

"Well then", Jessica was very cheerful this morning, "you must come and listen to Maxi play at the club. Lots of young people there."

Aisling arrived at the jazz club in the company of Max and Jessie. She was instantly excited by the bright lights of the exterior. Inside, Aisling and Jessie sat at the table very near the stage and Max left them to join the band. The tables all round the dance floor were filling up and there was a great air of expectation around the smoke filled club. The band came on to the stage and the music started – throbbing and sensuous. Aisling watched Max intently when he played his solo pieces with such passion. Aisling and Jessie smiled at each other as they watched a group of young women nearby applauding wildly and Max responded by playing enthusiastically towards them. He knew most of them as they came to listen to him every week. The enjoyment of that night was to be repeated many times for Aisling, sometimes going to the club with Jessie and more often, as time went by, going alone, sitting near the stage. When Jessie did not accompany Aisling to the club, she usually stayed at home where she lived with her father and Gus.

It was Christmas Day, Aisling and Jessie descended the steps, having been to Mass at the Cathedral. They emerged into a sunny frosty morning. Everything was covered with a light dusting of snow. The fairy lights in the streets and trees twinkled. People hurried past. The girls greeted each other "Merry Christmas".

"What a wonderful morning Aisling, so different to how I felt a few short years ago."

"Different?" Aisling was puzzled.

"I was married, Aisling."

"Married? Jessie I didn't know."

"I know you didn't, but now I'll tell you the whole sorry story."

They walked along, arm in arm, feeling warm in their long coats and fur lined boots. Aisling adjusted her hat and looked up at the sky.

"Oh, look at that sky, we're going to have more snow." Jessie laughed.

"How do you know by looking up at the sky?"

"I know" Aisling said wisely.

"I rely on the weather forecast myself" Jessie said.

"Now, about this story of my life so far, I was going to tell you. Do people disclose their innermost feelings at Christmas time? I think they do. What do you think?"

"Well, there are some poor creatures who have no one to disclose their innermost feelings to. Maybe they pray for the rest of us. But, tell me your story."

"Ok, when we came here form Chicago, Ray, who played the drums, came with us. He was considerably older than me, twenty years in fact. He was suave, sophisticated and drunk a lot of the time. I was young and impressionable, of course, blinded to all except his good looks and persuasive ways. My father disapproved of the relationship but I was defiant. The old, old story. We are all knowledgeable in hindsight, I suppose." Jessie shrugged.

"So where did you get married? Was it here at the Cathedral?"

"No, I'm afraid not. We went back to Chicago where Ray got a licence and we were married very quickly in the clothes we left New York in. So much for the white dress and coronet" Jessie whispered sadly.

"But we were happy living in a dingy apartment near where his sister was living at the time. I say 'happy'. It was for me and probably for him, when he was sober. But the alcohol took its toll, he played less and less and drank more and more."

"He was an alcoholic", Aisling said quietly.

"Oh, yes, long before I met him. His sister told me the whole story – how he married and divorced twice before. I began to feel lonely and isolated. I missed the family here and told him one evening that I would like to come back to visit them. He refused. You were right Aisling, the snow is falling thicker now. Still, we're nearly home. You and John will be coming to dinner later on, won't you?"

"Yes, of course" Aisling said hurriedly.

"Do you want to continue your story?"

"I think it was the last straw when one morning, Sunday it was, I heard shouting outside the Church. I knew his voice immediately and cowered down in the seat." She laughed.

"I can laugh now when I think about it, but it was frightening at the time. I contacted my father and he came and brought me back home."

"So what happened to Ray?"

"His health deteriorated and he died in hospital. My father and Gus went to the funeral."

"What an awful time it was for you, Jessie."

"It was."

They reached Jessie's apartment block and Aisling walked swiftly home a few blocks away. She was making her way to the elevator when Mario and Carla stepped out. "Aisling" they said in unison. "Merry Christmas" Carla said. We haven't seen you for so long. We are just going over to be with our cousins for the Christmas. Please, come and see us soon." "I will" Aisling promised. It was true. She hadn't seen them lately. She would love to go to the Opera with Mario sometime.

John and Aisling arrived at the apartment laden with Christmas gifts. They entered the hall where they were greeted by Jessie, Bill and Gus. Greetings over, they all streamed into the sitting room, which was almost overpowered by the large tree, decorated with lights and baubles. It was so welcoming and warm. They all sat round the dining room table and enjoyed a traditional meal – Max being conspicuous by his absence.

"Will Max be coming over later" Aisling was curious.

"My dear, when did that boy ever observe anything of tradition?

Bill said "Eh, Gus?"

Gus nodded, but hiding a smile.

"He knows Aisling is here, he'll be along later, I'm sure."

John was silent. Aisling felt good. She went into the kitchen where Jessie was busy with flaming the plum pudding.

"I'll help you with all this Jessie."

"Gus said that Max would be coming in later."

"Mmm", Jessie was concentrating on the pudding "but don't hold your breath."

They went into the dining room with the flaming pudding.

"Very impressive Jessie", John said admiringly.

The key turned into the front door lock and Max bounced into the dining room.

"Merry Christmas all". "The same to you Max".

"Merry indeed", Bill muttered.

Jessie and Aisling left the dining room having finished the meal. Max followed.

"We had such a crazy night last night".

He looked at one to the other, "Into the early hours in fact". He looked the worse for the wear - dishevelled, and unshaven.

"Aisling, you must come out and celebrate the New Year. Jessie doesn't do that anymore, so you Sis?"

"Well, yes I will" Aisling was delighted.

Aisling and Max celebrated the New Year in the club. It was more crowded, more noisy and more smokey than usual. The season's decorations were everywhere and fairy lights were strung around the room. At the stroke of midnight she was whisked from her seat, joined the crowd which formed a circle, held hands crossed and sang Auld Lang Syne along with the band. The song finished, she saw Max walking towards her, smiling. They embraced each other and kissed. "Happy New Year". All the couples around the floor did this and Aisling felt such intimacy as she looked at Max.

"Come on, Aisling, some champagne."

They sat at the table and drank the champagne, joined by some of the band and Max's friends.

"More champagne", Max was saying as he stood up waving the bottle.

Aisling looked at the laughing crowds swirling by - she felt she was floating with them. What a wonderful place to be and to be here with Max, but he was taken away into the crowd by the hoards of giggling girls.

"Come on Maxi".

When Aisling looked up again - the lights seemed to have dimmed and the crowds were leaving. The balloons which Aisling tried to catch earlier were limp and strewn across the floor. The people at her table had also gone and the band was silent. But once again, there was Max, smiling, striding across the floor.

"Come on Aisling, time to go home."

"Time to go home", Aisling repeated.

She tried to get up, but fell back down again. She looked at Max.

"Max, the room is spinning around."

"Come on Aisling, it's the champagne".

She got up and walked unsteadily and dreamily, linking Max's arm, to the waiting cab.

Aisling woke up, realising very quickly that she was in a strange room. She had been lying on an uncomfortable sofa, fully clothed. There was a cushion acting as a pillow - nothing else. She felt cold. The room was freezing cold. The walls were adorned with posters of jazz musicians dominated by a huge poster of Louis Armstrong. Of course, she must be in Max's apartment. She stood up and looked around for her shoes.

“So you’re awake. Coffee is what you need”.

Max was standing at what she thought was the kitchen door. Returning to the kitchen he poured two mugs of coffee.

“You were out for the count last night”.

Aisling found her shoes and followed him into the kitchen.

“Out .....?”

“Yes, you know, inebriated, drunk”.

He looked at her with a sarcastic smile and handed her the coffee. That smile - it was so different to last night. Suddenly she was irritated. Why was she here? Then she remembered. She was floating. She remembered last night. She remembered New Year’s Eve.

“I’ve got to go home right now”.

She felt the panic rising inside.

“Ok. I’m going back to the club later on, won’t you come?”

“No, I’m going home”.

Max shrugged.

It was still snowing. She reached her warm apartment. John was sitting by the sitting room window, reading.

"You and Jessie saw the New Year in in spectacular fashion I suppose?" "Yes, John", she said and retreated to her room. Her heart ached. She did not want to deceive him.

She had a shower, changed her clothes and lay on her bed. Yes, she saw the New Year in - in spectacular fashion - with Max. She would go down to the club again and see him and lose herself in his embrace. It was so lonely without him. She looked at the ceiling. She counted the flowers and leaves on the rose around the ceiling lights, the same pattern was repeated around the edge - she slept.

Aisling continued to visit the club where Max was playing - often staying with him and his friends to party long into the night. She came to work with John and Jessie less and less and they became very concerned for her. When she did come to work, she looked pale and unkempt and left early. Jessie expressed her concern to her once, telling her that John was worried for her welfare, but she shrugged it off.

"I'm okay. I'm with Max".

"Yes, Aisling, that's the trouble, he's my brother, but he cares for no one but himself".

Aisling was defensive.

"Of course he does, Jessie, he loves me. In fact I sang at the club last week, and he said I was wonderful and that you and John would be proud. He said that I sang like your mother used to sing". Jessie was silent.

Thinking that Jessie's silence was an indication for her to continue she said "We are going to Vegas to see Elvis. Have you seen him on TV? Isn't he wonderful? I know that John will want me to go. He wants me to be happy doesn't he? And I am. I must talk to my dear Father. I haven't seen much of him lately".

"Lately! It's been weeks if not months. Aisling, are you really aware of that? You come in here when it suits you - looking terrible I may add. What is it? Alcohol?"

"Really, Jessie" Aisling interrupted "a few drinks at the club".

She stared at Jessie, her eyes wild, her cheeks flushed.

"Maybe you should have a few drinks and come to the club sometimes".

Jessie ignored that comment.

"You really should go home and see John. Cousin Maimie visited some time ago and was asking about you".

Aisling looked startled.

"Who on earth is Cousin Maimie?"

"It's not for me to tell you. Your Father will tell you all about her I'm sure", Jessie said coldly.

Aisling left the office and headed towards Max's apartment. Cousin Maimie, she muttered. I have no cousins. Using the key that Max had given her she entered his apartment. Max was sitting on the sofa talking to a young woman.

"Hi Max. Got a drink? Who is this? Cousin Maimie?"

Max got up from the sofa and steered Aisling towards the kitchen. He looked agitated.

"What are you doing here this early in the day?"

Aisling nodded towards the sitting room.

"Is that Cousin Maimie?"

She looked seriously concerned.

"No, Aisling, that is not Cousin Maimie."

"Do you know Cousin Maimie, Max?"

"I met her once or twice."

"Oh, so I have a Cousin. Where's that drink Max?"

"Aisling, go home and talk to John."

"Max, you sound just like your sister."

In the cab, on the way home, Aisling thought of Max's indifference. He had not introduced her to his fair haired friend sitting on the sofa. Who was she and were there other 'friends'. She banished the thought from her mind.

No, that was not possible. He told her he loved her, didn't he?

At home, John was sitting in his usual chair by the window.

"Well, it's good to see you."

Aisling apologised for her absence and told John she had been with Max. Eager to change the subject –

"I hear I have a Cousin Maimie?"

"Yes, indeed, she is getting married again, I believe."

"Really".

Aisling was interested.

"Tell me about her."

John looked at her and Aisling noticed for the first time that he was looking pale and tired.

"Are you okay, John?"

"Yes, but I need to talk to you."

"Let's have some coffee and tell me about Cousin Maimie."

It was twilight time one fine spring evening. Aisling switched on all the lights around the room and set the cups down on the coffee table which divided the space between John and herself.

"Maimie", he mused, "she isn't really a cousin, you know. I remember her when we were children. She used to come with her parents to our house when my mother used to have her famous parties. She used to sit in a corner, watching everybody and not saying a word. Then, the next day, they would be all gone home, but as time went by, they came more frequently and stayed overnight sometimes. Gradually, Maimie would be left to stay with us. I remember once, one summer, she stayed with us during all the school holidays. My Mother said that it was fine because she was our cousin. Shortly after that my Mother married Colm and we went to live on the island."

John sipped his coffee.

"What happened to her after that?"

Aisling made herself comfortable by plumping up the cushions around her.

"Well, what a surprise. She turned up here shortly after I met your mother again in this City."

His voice had trailed almost to a whisper. Aisling felt his pain.

"John ....".

"Yes, indeed," he smiled at the memory of Cousin Maimie.

"No more sitting in a corner for her, she walked in here, brash as you like, said she was my cousin and introduced her new husband. She had been working as a waitress in Greenwich Village and had met him in the restaurant where she worked – not far from the theatre where he worked as an actor. She was so glad she could visit before they left for California the week after that."

"That's an amazing story, John. What did she look like then? She must have changed a lot when you saw her recently. What did she look like then?"

"She was tall with fair hair, striking, I suppose you would call it. Talkative and now, you ask? She has mellowed a bit. You will see for yourself when you meet her."

"So, John, in California …."

"No, it was not a happy marriage she said a few years afterwards. She wrote to us shortly after we were married saying that she was practically down and out and she desperately wanted to come home. So, of course, your Mother, being the loving and generous person she was, sent her the fare. She came back and stayed with us for a while. Yes, Aisling, before you ask, more coffee please."

Aisling poured, wanting to hear more of this intriguing story.

"Restless again, she went down to Lisdoonvarna one September."

"What", Aisling exclaimed, did she find …."

"Yes, a farmer from West Cork. Much older than she was."

They both laughed.

"She then wanted to get married in Rome, but he objected. He was unable to travel because of the arthritis in his hip."

"What a girl!"

Aisling was warming to her by the minute.

"The farm turned out to be a smallholding, but she remained there for ten years, after which time her husband died. Living alone was not a lifestyle for her, so she sold up and bought a small guesthouse in the nearest town, which is a Mecca for tourists."

"I suppose she was doing ok there?"

"Oh, yes – she thrived on the hustle and bustle I should imagine and apparently became quite the pillar of the community."

Aisling was confused.

"So, why is she back here again?"

"Well, she met many tourists in her guesthouse over the years and, yes, you've guessed it, that's where she met her future husband, and agreed to come back to the US with him."

"The wedding invitations have arrived,"

Jessie announced as John and Aisling came through the door of the office. Aisling tore open hers.

"The wedding will take place in California to one Irwin Foley in September."

She looked at Jessie.

"You don't seem too happy about it", she observed.

"Of course, it's a happy occasion." Jessie looked solemn, "but I also have sad news." Gus was taken into hospital last night. He was involved in an auto accident", she said quickly. "My Father is with him."

"What happened? How is he?"

The phone rang, Jessie answered. She looked stunned.

"Gus has just died."

Tears streamed down the girls' faces.

"Come on, right now," John ordered gruffly, belying his inner feelings.

"We are going to the hospital."

At the hospital, they found Bill looking utterly dejected. Jessie ran to him. Bill looked up showing his tear-stained face.

"He's gone, Jessie. My friend Gus."

They all gathered round him.

"We can't stay here Bill," John said gently, "let's go home."

John contacted all the members of the band and various people at the club. Gus's funeral was arranged in the following few days. It was to be attended by Gus's only family for many years, Bill, Jessie and his beloved Max, John and Aisling and of course all his friends at the jazz club. The band played their laments along the funeral route. Max was not among the mourners.

"A funeral and a wedding in such a short space of time," Aisling remarked on their way to the cemetery.

"C'est la vie", John said.

The California sun shone down on the happy couple in the small church in Los Angeles – Cousin Maimie and her new husband, Irwin Foley.

Irwin, who had travelled across the Pacific Ocean, visiting Australia, New Zealand and the Fiji Islands in search of ways to conquer the awful loneliness he felt after the death of his beloved wife. He enjoyed the trip, meeting wonderful people on the way, but nothing or nobody could take away the pain of his loss. "What could he do?" His mother had often talked about the County Cork. So, he would travel to Ireland, maybe meet some cousins there. It was three years since his last trip and friends encouraged him to go and try and find his relatives in Ireland. People who already had been there spoke highly of the warmth and hospitality of the people.

He checked into Maimie's guesthouse. Maimie was there to welcome him. She made sure that 'the lovely American gentleman' was shown into the best bedroom – the one with the en-suite shower room which she had installed for this year's 'season'.

The wedding reception was held on the front lawn of Irwin's house in the Californian hills. Only close friends and relatives were present, Aisling, John, Jessie and her father Bill, and Max along with some of Irwin's old friends. Max had brought his trumpet, as always, and was now playing to a small but appreciative audience over in the far corner of the lawn.

"There he is", Bill said to Aisling and others, pointing over to Max. "Never happier than when he is playing to his adoring fans."

The sun was sinking and some of the guests were leaving, once again congratulating the couple. Max had stopped playing and approached Aisling, who was sitting alone watching the sun go down.

"Come on, we are all going to Vegas."

Thinking that he meant the family, she jumped up.

"Oh, yes – who's going?"

"The friends I've made today, of course. You know, people I've been playing to."

She had seen the little circle of young people he now called his friends.

"Are you coming or not Aisling? They have transportation. It will be such a great drive through the desert."

Aisling said "I'll just go and tell John and the others."

"Oh, please hurry."

Max was impatient.

"We are going right now."

Aisling found John talking to Maimie and Irwin. She was excited, breathless.

"What's this?" John said, smiling, "Are you running the mile?"

"I'm going to Vegas with Max and his friends" she blurted out, and with that she hurried away.

She met Jessie and almost ran into her.

"I'm going to Vegas with Max," she was still breathless.

Jessie was startled.

"Call us, when you get there" she shouted to Aisling, who was now running across the lawn.

She found Max with six young people who were packing their car with various bags, suitcases and boxes into the trunk – four girls and three boys. The late evening was humid as they drove through the desert. Their spirits were high on the journey and they became more noisy as they consumed the beer.

"Wake up Aisling", Max was shouting.

She was dazed.

"What's happened?"

"We are stuck in the sand. The driver lost control – we've got to get this out."

After what seemed an age they pushed the car free. No one was fit to drive any further.

"Aisling, you've been sleeping most of the way, you drive."

Aisling got behind the wheel and drove steadily – all passengers now quiet or sleeping. They finally reached Vegas in the early hours of the morning, exhausted. Max was adamant that they check into a hotel immediately and then head off to the casinos.

"Got any money?" Max's familiar question to Aisling.

She rummaged in her bag.

"This is all I have, we left in such a hurry."

Max was already hurrying towards the tables. He gambled and lost. Then he went away to look for the others with Aisling trailing behind. They caught up with the others who had met old friends and said they were going to a party at the hotel.

"A party", Aisling exclaimed.

She joined the boisterous group of friends with Max leading the way. Down the Strip they went, laughing and some of them singing. Suddenly Aisling tripped on the kerb. Nobody seemed to have noticed. She called out "Max" as she fell.

It was just before dawn, the sky was semi dark and even with the street lights, outside the casino seemed grey compared to the constant bright lights inside. Chuck Mulcahy blinked. He was elated.

"I cannot believe the good fortune we had in there tonight. I think we are going to live for ever."

His brother, Bernard, agreed.

"Yea, it was Lady Luck smiling alright. I feel like walking to the hotel."

"A great walk" Chuck mocked, "just across the street."

The brothers, Chuck and Bernard Mulcahy were business partners who took time out every year to visit Vegas – to discuss business and family, but mostly to relax.

"Somebody's lost their shirt tonight"

Chuck laughed as they slipped off the kerb to cross the road,

“not only their shirt”,

Bernard laughed as they both peered at the bundle of clothes in the gutter.

“Wait a minute”, Chuck said, “I think they’ve moved.”

“Oh, please” Bernard scoffed, “you didn’t drink that much tonight.”

“No, seriously, it’s a young woman.”

By now a crowd had gathered.

“What’s happened? Is she dead?”

They were both kneeling beside her now. They looked at each other.

“She has a weak pulse”, Bernard said.

“Get the police – get an ambulance,” someone in the crowd shouted.

The paramedics, having examined Aisling, lifted her on to a stretcher and into the ambulance. It sped away, sirens screaming. The crowd scattered.

“No one lives forever”, Bernard said soberly.

Aisling could hear muffled voices. She opened her eyes to see John holding both her hands and Jessie and Bill looking anxious.

"Oh, my dear", John squeezed her hands.

"How are you feeling?"

Aisling managed a weak smile, "I'm okay, but my head hurts."

"I'm not surprised" Jessie said, "you took a nasty fall."

"Oh, yes, the fall".

Memories came rushing back.

"Where is Max?"

"He is still in Vegas", Jessie reassured her.

Aisling closed her eyes again. Jessie and Bill exchanged glances. John kept looking at Aisling. She opened her eyes.

"How long have I been here?"

"Just a day or two", John patted her hand.

"Doctor says you had concussion, so they kept you here for observation – home again very soon I expect."

Aisling was allowed home the next day.

"Lots of rest", doctor said.

"Most certainly", John smiled.

Back in New York, Aisling was quiet, reflecting on the events in Las Vegas. Max had left her. Did he know what happened? She cried bitterly. Yes, he doesn't care. He had left her. How heartless he is.

"He left me to die," she wailed.

In the weeks and months that followed, Aisling and Jessie became close. Max was hardly mentioned, except when he appeared on TV playing in Las Vegas. The girls worked together every day under John's guidance, and John was heartened that Aisling was doing well and learning the business. He had hinted more than once that he would soon be ready to retire. He was looking forward to playing some golf with Bill, Jessie's father. Bill also wanted some relaxation. He had not played at the club since Max's departure. So, both men played golf. John mostly at weekends, and Bill, having more time on his hands, played quite frequently and also played the piano, occasionally, at the golf club. They became engaged in the social life there.

The Christmas Dinner and Dance was such an occasion, attended by John, Bill, Aisling and Jessie. There, they met Mario and Carla along with some of their relatives who were over from Italy. The evening was lively and enjoyable. The achievements of the golfers during the year were read out and duly applauded. Mario and Aisling danced to the beat of the music. Aisling enjoyed every step and Mario was struggling. He had amassed some weight since they had last met. Finally, he mopped his brow and finished the dance.

"Aisling, the opera still awaits you. When will you come?"

Aisling was delighted at having met Mario again.

"I would love to go to the opera with you, Mario."

"Good, I'll be performing next week."

John, Aisling and Carla went to the theatre to see Mario performing as the Commendatore in Mozart's 'Don Giovanni'. Carla had seen him perform many times and commented

"He is better every time."

She was so happy that he was at home at this time because the operatic company travelled all over the United States. But he would be leaving New York again soon, as they were travelling to California.

In the spring of that year, John announced his retirement. Sitting at the breakfast table with Aisling –

"Aisling, my dear, I've decided to retire."

That means, of course, that the business will be yours, but I intend to speak to Jessica and offer her one half."

He looked very seriously at Aisling.

"Do you agree?"

"Yes, yes, I agree, of course."

She was now lost for words.

"I've been contemplating this for some time now, as you probably know. It is for the best. Jessica and yourself make a good team. I shall speak to her tomorrow – better still, I'll make it this afternoon".

Jessie was flushed with excitement.

"A half share in the business, John, and with Aisling. I would be delighted and honoured."

"You are well capable of running the business, Jessica, and I know that Aisling will be grateful that you have accepted. I shall tell all the staff in the morning."

Sitting in the Sitting Room a week later, Aisling looked at John.

"Are you enjoying your retirement, John?"

"I am, indeed, glad to have shifted the burden onto young shoulders," John smiled.

"It's no burden, I'm enjoying the challenge and it's good to be working with Jessie. But I have my own announcement to make." John looked concerned.

"What announcement, Aisling?"

"Well, you probably noticed that Mario and I are seeing a lot of each other. Actually, he has asked me to marry him."

She looked at her Father expectantly.

"Well, my dear, this is good news. He is a fine young man, even if we don't see much of him on stage," he said teasingly.

"Unlike usual times," Aisling chimed in "where it would be difficult not to see him."

She smiled at the thought of Mario's bulky frame.

"But he is leaving for California with the opera company quite soon, not before he comes to see you, I might add. He would like me to travel with him and stay for a few days or so. It would also give us a chance to visit Maimie and Irwin whom I have not seen since I left their wedding party so abruptly – maybe invite them to our own ....."

"Yes, yes" John interrupted, lifting up his hand in protest.

"Not so fast, young lady. Let me talk to Mario."

John was in the Sitting Room awaiting Mario's arrival – right on time the door bell rang. Aisling answered and they both came in to greet John. The men shook hands.

"Drinks?" Aisling offered.

"What will it be?"

"A beer for me" John replied,

"Mario?"

"I'll have a beer, thanks."

"The ball game is on TV," John said.

"Oh, good" Mario said.

They both settled down to watch the game and Aisling returned with the beers, leaving immediately.

In view of the Golden Gate Bridge, Mario placed a diamond solitaire engagement ring on Aisling's left hand ring finger.

"Mario, it's beautiful, it fits perfectly. How did you ….."

Mario held Aisling's two hands and kissed them.

"I am so happy. Can we name the day as soon as possible?"

"Wait, wait" Aisling said, laughing.

"Let's enjoy our engagement time. Let's enjoy being together here in the sun, in sunny California."

As they walked along the sea shore Aisling extended her left arm several times to admire her ring.

"Look how it sparkles in the sun. We must go and visit Irwin and Maimie and tell them our good news."

"Who?"

"Oh, you don't know them."

She then told him their story, who Maimie was and how she and Irwin met. Mario was intrigued.

"Yes, I would like to meet them. We must find time between performances."

The visit to Maimie and Irwin was brief. They welcomed the newly engaged couple with open arms. Maimie looked at Mario –

"My, what a big man" she exclaimed, as he filled the door space.

The ring was admired over and over again, and Irwin, who was usually reserved, asked –

"When is the wedding to be?"

Mario squared his shoulders, and standing up to his full height,

"as soon as possible."

"In New York, I presume?"

"Oh, yes, where the family is

and looking at both Maimie and Irwin,

"you are on top of the list of invitations."

"We certainly will look forward to that."

In New York, Aisling, Jessie and John decided to visit the theatre where Mario was performing. John sat comfortably in his seat with Aisling and Jessie sitting either side of him. The lights went down. Slowly the curtain rose. There was an air of expectancy all around. John began to shuffle his feet and he seemed to be uncomfortable. As Aisling looked uneasily at him, he fell sideways on her shoulder. "John", Aisling looked at Jessie, who immediately left the theatre to seek help.

In the hospital the two girls waited for news. The doctor came, shook his head. There was nothing they could do. He had died instantly.

Aisling went back to work with Jessie, taking over her part of the business. She worked long hours while telling Mario that she wanted to get married as soon as possible. Mario was taken aback.

"But, my darling, it's so soon after John....."

"I'm on my own now, I don't want to be on my own. I want to be with you all the time."

"But, you are".

"No, I am not. I don't see you enough. Please, Mario, let's get married straight away" she pleaded.

Jessie talked to Aisling when she told her that she was very anxious to get married soon.

"Getting married in the Church will take time to organise."

"No," Aisling shook her head, "I don't want to wait."

"Would you not want a great white wedding?"

"No, I don't. I'm going to ask Mario if we can do this quickly, in Vegas maybe."

As Mario had contemplated his wedding, he thought he might like to honeymoon in Sydney, Australia. The new Opera House has been designed and was already being built.

So, the wedding took place in Las Vegas as Aisling so much wanted and they were very happy to spend their honeymoon in Sydney as Mario had arranged.

On arriving at their hotel it was evening. Feeling exhausted after their long journey, they wished to get to their bedroom suite quickly. Going to the lift with their luggage, it was full. Aisling said to wait for the lift to come back, but Mario was impatient. He walked towards the stairs carrying one bag. He struggled up one flight with Aisling close behind.

"It's ok, we can have the rest of the luggage sent up."

Turning the corner towards the next flight, Mario went up three steps and tripped and fell over the bag.

"Mario, that bag is too heavy."

She tried to lift the bag but he was lying on it and did not move.

"Mario, Mario" she looked at him – his face was blue.

People were surrounding them suddenly.

"What is it?" Aisling asked.

They were looking at Mario.

"He's not breathing" she heard someone say "Mario".

Aisling screamed.

"No, it's John."

She threw herself on to him. She pulled at his face, his arms.

"John, come back, come back." She felt strong arms pulling her away. She sank down, down into the darkness.

She opened her eyes. She had come out of the darkness, lying in a bed with people around her.

"Aisling, can you hear me?"

She saw everyone but could not speak. She closed her eyes again.

"Aisling, can you hear me?"

She opened her eyes again and saw a nurse bending over her. She could not be sure how long she had been in that state.

Slowly she was recovering. She spoke eventually to the nurse – Nurse Judy who had been looking after her. She walked around the ward of the hospital. She ate and drank a little, always encouraged by Judy.

"You must come out and sit in the garden."

"But it's winter isn't it?"

"No" Judy smiled. Down here it is summertime."

"Down here?"

"You're in Australia."

"Yes, I know."

She sat in the garden every day, watching the other patients walking by and looking at the birds, the Ibis … walking sedately around and the Kookaburra sitting in a tree opposite her seat. Every day he perched himself there. Judy came and talked to her.

"That patient sitting over there, Judy, what's his name?"

"His name is John".

"John" Aisling whispered.

"He sits on that seat every day, looking down on the ground – for hours it seems and then he goes back into the hospital again. Maybe he finds peace sitting there."

"Yes, maybe he does, he 's been here a long time."

"Judy, I want to show you something. I wrote this poem."

She produced a paper from her bag, and handed it to Judy.

The torment of words
All jumbled up
As usual, screaming
But not here
Down in the garden
Sitting on the seat

The whisperings at night
Frantic and fierce
Where are you now?
But not here,
Down in the garden
Sitting on the seat

The TV and radio
Blaring it out
Who are you now?
But not here
Down in the garden
Sitting on the seat

Where am I? Who am I?
Where the voices?
Not here – down in the garden, sitting on the seat.

Judy gave her back the poem.

"Aisling that is so beautiful. You really have improved greatly in the past few weeks. I believe you will be ready to go home soon. You know, it will be good for you, to walk the familiar streets when you do return home. You came from New York didn't you?"

"Yes".

Judy returned to the ward. Aisling sat alone on the seat watching the Kookaburra. Yes, she would walk through the streets and the old roads of her childhood. The Kookaburra flew away. She watched him go, higher and higher.

Mary, Lily and Josie had finished breakfast. Josie had gone upstairs, Lily was clearing away the dishes and Mary sat in her armchair by the window and picked up her knitting. Lily mopped her brow.

"It's going to be a scorcher today. I'll just go and open the French door to let in a bit of air."

She came back in, resumed clearing the dishes and looked at Mary.

"When is that jumper going to be finished? It looks big enough to fit Fin McCool."

"Yes, I know" Mary smiled.

"But Josie has put on a bit of weight lately. His sister Nancy and her husband want him to go and live with them. They were here yesterday asking him. I don't think he's too keen, but I think it would be better for him."

"Oh, yes, I think so too."

Lily was moving into the small kitchen.

"He's been with us now for how many years?"

"Well, ages. Going out every morning, going up to the square in that old Hackney Cab. I'm sure he sits in it half the time, sleeping with his hat over his eyes. Here he is now. He seems to get noisier on the stairs since we took up that ragged old carpet."

"God bless all here" a male voice boomed out from the open front door.

"You too, Sir" Josie replied, and called to Lily on his way out.

Mary put her knitting down and her arthritric hands gripped the arms of the chair. Lily stood at the kitchen door and faced Mary. They started at each other.

"It can't be" Lily whispered, shaking her head.

Quickly composing herself, she rushed out on to the hall. She saw a white haired, white bearded man standing there, tall, slim, tanned and wearing grey trousers and a white open-necked shirt.

"Well" he said smiling, showing even white teeth.

"Is it yourself, Lily? You haven't changed one bit."

Lily was silent but thought

"You haven't changed either, with your silver tongue."

"Mary is in here" she said.

"May I come in?" Tom Quinn asked in a subdued voice.

They entered the room, "Mary, someone to see you." Mary already knew.

She stood up, holding out both hands as Tom walked over. He took her hands in his. "Mary" he said. "Tom." The years raced by between them.

"Come and sit down here at the table."

They sat opposite each other. She looked at him. He needs to sit down. He looks weary, still the handsome Tom. He has come home. My prayers .... She had so many questions, but couldn't ask.

"How are you, Tom?" she asked simply.

"Oh, Mary, how am I? I'm here with you. It's all I ever wanted. I have travelled so far. I lived in Australia, Mary, I went from riches to rags and back again. It was the gambling, as you well know. I lost everything. I thought I would never see you again. It was then that I promised that I would never gamble again. It wasn't easy, Mary, and it took me a few years, but now I'm here."

He paused. His Mary, listening patiently, always dignified. He lowered his eyes and his voice – and our child, Mary?

Mary stood up,

“Oh, Patsy, she’s fine, working over there in London.”

“Would you like a cup of tea Tom?”

“I would”.

He followed her into the kitchen. He looked around.

“Mary, you and Lily and Patsy have lived here for such a long time – it’s an old house. I’ll build you a new place.”

“No, Tom” she shook her head, “we are happy enough here.”

“I want to, Mary, I can afford to do it, for yourself and Lily.” He faltered – “and maybe myself.”

“Where is Lily?”

“She’s gone upstairs to Pièrre.”

“Who’s Pièrre?”

“Her husband”.

“She got married” he exclaimed.

Mary smiled at his look of surprise.

“And who is this Pièrre? Anyone I know?”

"Oh, yes, you remember Jack de Vere? Well, that's Pièrre.

"She married Jack De Vere did she?"

They carried their tea into the dining room.

"So, Mary, why is he called Pièrre?"

"Well, Tom, you remember that Lily was always in the amateur dramatics ..."

Lily saw Mary extend her hands to Tom, she left, shutting the dining room door, threw off her shoes and ran upstairs. "Pièrre, Pièrre". Pièrre emerged from the bathroom, wiping his face with a towel.

"I have hardly time to finish shaving, what is it now?"

They moved into the bedroom.

"You'll never guess who's downstairs? It's Tom Quinn – back from wherever he was in the world."

"Be the hokey, Lily, that's great news now."

"I don't know – if I were Mary, I'd throw him out, coming back here after all this time."

"Ah, but Lily, you are not Mary. You wouldn't throw me out, sure you wouldn't. I think he went to Australia. We should have gone there when we were young."

"You would not go anywhere, you wouldn't leave here and you know that, Jack De Vere."

Yes, alright Lily.

"Tom Quinn was a great fella, you know, but he liked to gamble."

"Ah sure, we all have our weaknesses, I suppose."

"Well, hurry up and get dressed and go downstairs and meet him, seeing as you like him so much."

They both went into the dining room. Tom stood up and greeted Pièrre. They shook hands warmly.

"Begod, now Tom, it's good to see you." Tom smiled broadly.

"Likewise I'm sure. I hear you made an honest women of herself" nodding towards Lily.

"I did, faith."

"You'll all want something to eat" Lily said as she moved towards the kitchen.

The two men sat at the able with Mary.

"You've done a lot of travelling, I'd say Tom."

Lily left the kitchen, coming through the dining room.

"I'm going across to Bessie's to get the milk."

Bessie's was a small shop across the street which sold groceries and bric-a-brac.

"Hello, Bessie, lovely day. I'm in a hurry. I've just come in to get the milk."

"Well there's no hurry on me" Bessie said as she reached for the milk, "business is slack. Ah sure, it's the same everywhere. The country is going to the dogs."

Bessie O'Toole sat her large body in the chair by the window, which was her habit of doing. From there she could observe all the comings and goings in the street.

"Here's your change Lily. I saw a man going into your place as Josie was going out on his way up to the square. I thought I knew him, but I couldn't be sure."

"Oh that was Tom Quinn."

Bessie watched her crossing the street. Tom Quinn, he was a bit of a 'wan' she thought.

Mag tied the dog outside and came in –

"I haven't seen you for a long time Mag. How are you now?"

"Oh, Bessie, the old rheumatism is killing me. I'm not too bad today with the good weather, but I still have to wear me shawl. I thought I'd come out and get the loaf of bread and here – put an ounce in it today."

She handed Bessie a small, well worn lidded tin.

"It keeps me going – you know yourself."

Bessie nodded. She got the bread, leaving it on the counter and searched underneath.

"Here you are, Mag, your ounce of snuff. Not many people are taking it these days."

"Thanks Bessie, but you know what they say 'old habits die hard'."

"Speaking of old habits" – Bessie was looking out of the window. The man across the street has a habit of coming and going."

"Who?

Tom Quinn, Who else?"

Mag put the bread and the snuff in her bag.

"He was a fine looking man" she said, shuffling her shoulders.

"Oh, there's poor Guess looking in. He wants me to go now."

Bessie craned her neck towards the door.

"I suppose he does. Funny name for a dog though."

"I'll tell you now how that happened. Did I tell you before? When Billie got him, he used to sit outside with him sometimes. People passing said 'That's a lovely dog, Billie, what's his name?' "Guess" Billie would say and they would say Spot or Rover and give different names.

'Don't know Billie, what's his name, Guess?' and they would move away. She laughed, "Billie used to love that. I'll say goodbye to you."

She untied the dog.

"Come on, Guess, we're going home."

Guess carried the bag in his mouth and they walked slowly up the street.

A tall, thin man appeared at the door leading on to the kitchen at the back of the shop.

"Is she gone – Mag or Maggie? It's time you closed for lunch."

"Yes, I'll close the door now."

Sitting at the kitchen table, eating the cheese sandwiches that her brother, Matt, had prepared, Bessie explained,

"No, her name isn't Maggie – its Mags."

"What's the difference?"

"Oh, a big difference. Her real name is Magdalene."

"Oh, is it and what's the dog's name?"

"Guess"

"I can't guess. Imagine asking me to guess a dog's name. What's his name, anyway?"

“Guess”.

“Oh, alright, you are not going to tell me. Do you want more tea? There’s two tomatoes if you want them.”

Patsy arrived at Euston Station, London, having travelled on the ferry from Dublin and on the night train from Holyhead. Her Uncle Brian and Aunt Lena were there to meet her. They put her one piece of luggage into the boot of their Morris Minor and drove to their home.

Disappointment ensued when she was unable to find a job.

Giving this some thought, she decided to enter the convent. She would write to the Reverend Mother at her nearest convent and ask for an interview. She arrived at the convent, wearing her best navy blue suit and white blouse, with the gold cross and chain, which her mother had given her before she left, around her neck. The convent was a large building with St Gerards Primary School in the same grounds. A young nun answered the door bell.

“Good morning”, she smiled, as she ushered Patsy into a small room on the ground floor.

“I’ll tell Reverend Mother that you’re here.”

The room was sparsely furnished and immaculately kept. Presently, the Reverend Mother entered, tall, thin, as Patsy would have put it ‘very cross looking’.

“Good morning Patricia, take a seat”, pointing to one of the armchairs while she herself sat on the seat opposite.

Patsy sat down, feeling apprehensive, feeling like she was back in school again.

"I see from your letter that you would like to become a postulant."

"I would, Mother."

"When did you decide this, Patricia?"

"Well, Mother, I left Galway about a month ago. I'm staying with my Uncle Brian and Aunt Lena, hoping to start work soon, but so far I haven't had any luck. I'm sleeping on the sofa in their sitting room, because the two children are in the other bedroom and it is not too comfortable, I can tell you Mother."

"No, I'm sure it isn't" Reverend Mother said sympathetically.

Encouraged by the Reverend Mother's tone, she went on – "I'd like to come in here, because I'd have a roof over my head and a decent bed to lie in."

"So you would like to enter the convent to get a roof over your head and a decent bed to lie in?"

"Yes, Mother, but I could work too."

"What work would you like to do?"

"Well, I don't know really, but I could do the cleaning, for a start. I used to do the cleaning at home, especially on a

Saturday morning. I did a lot of cleaning, the stairs – well there are a lot of stairs. Often, when I finished, Josie O'Hare, the taxi driver, who stayed with us for years, used to come down, with his big boots and make such a noise. He is so fat, Mother, I used to think he's going to slip one day, bang his head on the hallstand there at the bottom of the stairs and fall down and kill himself."

"Well, I hope that won't happen" Reverend Mother said dryly.

She paused.

"Patricia, I don't think you are ready to enter the convent just yet. But, I have a friend who is the manager in one of the hotels in the Strand. He may be able to find a nice position for you there."

"What strand, Mother?"

"The Strand here in the West End."

"I didn't know that there was a strand in London".

"Aisling and myself used to go out to the Silver Strand on Sundays during the summer. A lot of people from the town used to go out swimming and kids playing in the sand."

"Oh, it's not that kind of strand, Patricia. It's the name of a place."

"Well" Reverend Mother said, standing up, "It's nice to meet you. I will write to you as soon as I hear from Mr Naughton in the Strand."

"Thank you, Mother. My Father used to work in some hotel in London."

"Oh, which one, do you know?"

"No, I don't. He left home when I was small."

"Left home?"

"Yes, Mother, I don't know where he is, but my Uncle says he thinks he's in Australia. I wish he would come home."

"Maybe he will soon, with the help of God. God Bless, Patricia."

"Goodbye Mother."

Having finished their meal of scrambled eggs, toast and homemade bread, Tom left to go to his hotel and said he would return later to take Patsy's phone call. She telephoned every Friday evening at 8 pm and Mary took the call from Mr and Mrs Spencer's phone. They were a retired couple who had recently returned from Malta and lived next door.

Sitting back around the table – "I still can't believe he's back," Lily looked at Mary and Pierre. "But will he stay, that's what I'm wondering?"

"Well, he might" Mary said quietly.

"He has offered to build a house for us."

"What!" Lily exclaimed, "A new house, and what did you say to that?"

"I don't know. We are quite happy here, aren't we?"

"Quite happy here, look at that kitchen with a range that's as old as the hills, and the bathroom with the rickety pipes – this draughty old place, freezing cold in the winter."

"What do you think Pièrre?"

"Well, a new place would be nice, right enough."

'Árd na Gréinne' was the name of the guest house in Salthill now occupied by Tom, Mary, Lily, Pièrre, Patsy and her husband, Mr Naughton and their daughter Gráinne. It was the early 1960s and tourism was thriving.

That first summer, they were all very busy with their guests filling the house. Mary and Tom were waiting for their house to be completed. It was not too far away and they hoped to move in my Christmas. Lily and Pierre would stay helping Patsy and Mr Naughton, while continuing with their amateur dramatics when possible.

Going through her papers one rainy day in October, Mary showed Patsy a letter from Aisling.

"I received this some time ago, before we moved here. I did reply, but I haven't heard a word since."

Patsy read the letter.

"She was engaged to be married", Aisling had written, and shortly after that, her father, John, had died suddenly. Patsy finished reading.

"That is so sad," she told her mother.

"I will write to her now and invite her to come back and stay with us for a while. I think she would come and maybe bring her fiancée too. We have so much catching up to do."

She became more enthusiastic as she spoke.

"Yes, I know she would be surprised and delighted to meet Mr Naughton and Gráinne." "We would all love to see her again," Mary caught Patsy's enthusiasm.

"That's settled then."

Patsy sat down at the table and wrote a long letter to her friend – My dear Aisling ....

Patrick J McDonagh

An bonn a bhuaigh Peait na Máistreása ag na Cluichí Tailteann i 1924

www.ingramcontent.com/pod-product-compliance
Lightning Source LLC
Chambersburg PA
CBHW070609310726
48982CB00001B/29

* 9 7 8 1 9 0 8 4 4 7 8 6 9 *